ENDORSEMENT

We often fail in our relationships with the people that mean the most in life—our wives and children. As men, we are challenged and driven to succeed at work. It is not that we intend to neglect our wives and children; it's that no one teaches us the skills of being a godly husband and father. For many of us, we simply do not know what to do.

Every Man a Warrior will arm you to win in the battles you face as husband and father. In the context of the scriptures and other men, it will guide you into understanding the specific critical issues in both roles. It will penetrate to the heart of the core concepts of caring for your wife and training your young children and teens—not just with knowledge, but with applications that grow the relationships. This study is not theoretical, but practical and encouraging.

I wish I had known these lessons in the early years of my marriage. It would have equipped me to do so much better as a husband and father. This study is a must for every man at any age. The material is tried and tested. It works! It is never too late to start building a better family!

Jerry E. White, Ph.D.
International President Emeritus
Chairman, U.S. Board of Directors, The Navigators

Every Man a Warrior

Helping Men Succeed in Life

Book 2

Marriage and Raising Children

By Lonnie Berger

EVERY MAN A WARRIOR is a ministry of The Navigators.

The Navigators are an interdenominational, nonprofit Christian organization, dedicated to discipling people **to know Christ and to make Him known**. *The Navigators have spiritually invested in people for over seventy-five years, coming alongside them one-on-one or in small groups to study the Bible, develop a deeper prayer life, and memorize the Scripture. Our ultimate goal is to equip men and women to fulfill the Great Commission of Matthew 28:19 to* **"Go and make disciples of all nations."** *Today, tens of thousands of people worldwide are coming to know and grow in Jesus Christ through the various ministries of The Navigators. Internationally, over 4,000 Navigator staff of 64 nationalities are serving in more than 100 countries.*

Learn more about The Navigators at www.navigators.org.

EVERY MAN A WARRIOR, BOOK 2: MARRIAGE AND RAISING CHILDREN

ISBN: 978-1-935-65123-9

Some of the anecdotal illustrations in this book are true to life and are included with permission of the persons involved. All other illustrations are composites of real situations, and any resemblance to people living or dead is coincidental.

Printed in the United States of America.

2 3 4 5 6 7 8 9 10 / 17 16 15 14 13 12

You may download and reproduce any of the resources from the website EveryManAWarrior.com. These have been provided by the author for your benefit.

Helping Men Succeed in Life

EVERY MAN A WARRIOR is a discipleship course designed to help men succeed in life. It is for men who want to become the warriors God intends, not living lives of mediocrity, but maturing and becoming equipped in the areas where men fight and need to win.

These areas include:

- Walking with God
- Marriage
- Raising Children
- Managing Money
- Going Through Hard Times
- Work
- Sex and Moral Purity
- Making Your Life Count

Overview of the *Every Man a Warrior* Series

EVERY MAN A WARRIOR is a discipleship Bible Study series for men comprised of three books. Here is how the course is put together:

Book 1 Walking with God
The first nine lessons of EVERY MAN A WARRIOR develop the essential skills of discipleship. These skills are: Having a Quiet Time, Meditating on Scripture, Prayer, and Application of the Word. These skills are then applied to the topics in the next two books. It is important that all men go through Book 1 before starting Books 2 and 3. Book 1 includes the EVERY MAN A WARRIOR verse pack and all course verses.

Book 2 Marriage and Raising Children
These eight lessons give practical help and a biblical outlook on both Marriage and Raising Children. It comes with a special emphasis on raising teenagers. These lessons have profoundly impacted the lives of men wanting to become better husbands and fathers.

Book 3 Money, Sex, Work, Hard Times, and Making Your Life Count
Book 3 has ten lessons that bring scriptural application to the issues of Money, Work, Sex and Moral Purity, Going Through Hard Times, and how to Make Your Life Count. After family, these are the issues that most consume a man's life and where he needs to succeed.

Single men may choose to use only Books 1 and 3.

How to Use This Study

Book 2 of the *EVERY MAN A WARRIOR* series is designed primarily for married men and those who have children or are expecting them. However, a number of single men have used this material and were blessed by it. If you have not completed Book 1, it is important that you do so. Much of the content in Book 2 depends on the foundational skills taught in *Book 1.*

In a Small Group

Using *EVERY MAN A WARRIOR* in a small group of four to six men is optimum. These groups normally meet in the evening. Some groups have met successfully early on Saturday mornings or during the week before work. A time slot of ninety minutes is needed for groups. *Some of the lessons are long and may require two weeks to adequately discuss the material.*

One-on-One

This study can also be used to disciple men one-on-one, such as over lunch, and can be accomplished in sixty minutes.

A Men's Sunday School Class

Book 2 can be used in a Sunday school class. However, because of the length of the lessons, most will take two weeks to complete depending on the time allotted for your class. That's okay. Because of the importance of these two topics—marriage and raising children—we do not want to rush through the material. In fact, these lessons may be some of the most important Bible studies you will ever do.

Groups that meet in a Sunday school class will need to pair off and share Quiet Times and review verses in groups of two in order to save time. Then the whole group can come back together to read the stories and discuss the lesson.

Always start the second week of the lesson by reviewing verses and sharing Quiet times. These disciplines are the core of your walk with God and are the most effective tools we have to bring about transformation. The longer you are in an accountability group, the deeper these spiritual disciplines will take root in your life.

How Every Man a Warrior Came About

EVERY MAN A WARRIOR comes from more than thirty years of discipleship experience while on staff with The Navigators. Over these years Lonnie Berger has worked to disciple, mentor, counsel, or train hundreds of men. The stories used in *EVERY MAN A WARRIOR* are all true. The names and some of the details have been changed to protect confidentiality and privacy.

Note to Leaders

Be sure to read The Leader's Guide on pages 13-14, before your first meeting.

The first page of each lesson is for you, the leader. It is important to follow the Leader's Guide even if you have led other Bible studies. It has come from two years of field testing and is designed to help your group succeed. For example, some men find the disciplines of Quiet Times and Scripture memory hard to do and want to skip those parts of the course. ***Following the Leader's Guide will insure that these items are not left out and makes the Leader's Guide the course disciplinarian, not you!*** Not all groups make it and it is normal to have some men drop from the course. Using the Leader's Guide gives you the greatest potential to have a successful group.

CONTENTS

BOOK 2

Special Note on Book 2

Some of the lessons in Book 2 are long and may require two weeks to adequately discuss the material. Always start the second week of the lesson by reviewing verses and sharing Quiet Times. These disciplines are the core of your walk with God and are the most effective tools we have to bring about transformation. The longer you are in an accountability group, the deeper these spiritual disciplines will take root in your life. Also, the person that leads the first half of the study should lead the second week as well.

FOREWORD

Congratulations! You have finished Book 1: the discipleship section of *EVERY MAN A WARRIOR.* Now you possess skills to have an effective Quiet Time, memorize verses, pray, and meditate on the Scripture. *These skills needed to be built into your life before addressing the areas where we as men fight and need to win.*

In the movie *Fireproof,* firefighter Caleb Holt, played by Kirk Cameron, is a hero—having rescued people from imminent death. But his marriage is going up in smoke. For me, the classic line in this film is, *"You will risk your life to save someone you don't even know, but you won't fight to save your own marriage!"*

The truth is that Captain Holt did not know what to do! Like many of us, he needed someone to help him discover how to fight for his marriage. That's the purpose of *EVERY MAN A WARRIOR.*

Gentlemen, you are going to learn how to fight. In Book 2, you are going to get trained and equipped to:

- *fight for your marriage and your relationship with your wife;*
- *fight for deeper connections with your children and more effectively give them training and preparation for their lives.*

We will make these topics our focal point for Quiet Times, Scripture memory, meditation, and Bible study. We will explore foundational biblical passages and target practical application. If you do the work, you will come out of this course a better man—more highly skilled to win the battles you face in life.

Book 2 will deal with some potentially sensitive areas of your life. *Remember, any personal information shared in this group is confidential and not to be shared with anyone, even your spouse.*

Leader's Guide to

LESSON 1 FILLING UP GAPS

NOTE TO NEW LEADERS

You can download the Leader's Guide from the website *www.EveryManAWarrior.com* to make it easier to follow while leading the lesson. It is important to follow the Leader's Guide while leading the lesson. While some items are the same each week, others are special, one-time instructions that will negatively impact the study if missed. These items are marked with a star. ★

FILLING UP GAPS

✓ Break into pairs and recite your verses from Book 1 to each other.

✓ Sign off on the *Completion Record.*

✓ Open the session with prayer.

✓ Go around the room, asking each man to share one Quiet Time.

✓ Read the *Foreword,* if you have not done so all ready.

✓ Begin reading the lesson paragraph by paragraph.

✓ Pages 17-26: Ask each of the questions on these pages. Depending on time, have two to four people give their answer. Try to include everyone.

✓ Page 25: Have each man share his *Points to Remember.*

✓ Page 26: Read the *Assignment* together. Have them place Genesis 2:18 in the front pocket of their *EMAW Verse Pack.* Encourage the men to start working on the other marriage verses as well.

★✓ *Have your Quiet Time in these passages this next week: John 13:2-15; Matthew 20:20-28; John 12:23-28; and 1 Corinthians*

13:1-13. From now on we will have our Quiet Times on passages that apply to the topic we are studying.

✓ End in group prayer using the *WAR* method we learned in Book 1. Pray for your wives and marriages and through any changes you need to make to be the husband God wants you to be.

Filling Up Gaps

It was Saturday afternoon when my phone rang. Ted was on the other end, asking if I would speak to his wife, Cindy, for a moment.

I had just met Ted and Cindy at a weekly prayer meeting. They were in their late fifties with grown children. I had introduced myself and asked if they would be part of my intercessory prayer team for the ministry. They wanted to know more about the ministry, so we spent a few minutes talking. That had been just two weeks ago.

When I told Ted I'd be glad to speak to Cindy, I did not know she was crying. With loud sobs and deep pain, she cried into the phone, *"I want a divorce!"*

I was shocked. I timidly asked what had happened. She calmed down a little and said she was sick and tired of being married to this man. The marriage had not turned out like she had hoped—and she ended with a rather loud declaration, *"And he won't change!"*

Ted came back on the phone, and we set up a time for me to meet him after work. We met at a local cafe and I began to ask questions.

Ted and Cindy had met in college and got married. Even though Ted had his Ph.D. in molecular biology and an excellent résumé, they had struggled financially. During their first ten years of marriage, Ted had been laid off from two prestigious, well-paying pharmaceutical jobs because of buyouts or budget cuts. After each layoff, Ted had been unemployed for over a year. Both times, Cindy, who came from a wealthy family, had gone back to work to pay the bills. She felt angry that Ted could not keep his job, and as a young mother she had hated being away from the kids.

During his first layoff, the couple started attending church. Both had invited Christ into their lives. They had spent the last twenty years actively involved in their church. Outwardly, they were living the American dream.

They had a beautiful home, and Ted's current job paid over $100,000. Yet their marriage was about to explode.

At the cafe, I asked Ted what was happening in his marriage. He responded by listing how Cindy always had unrealistic expectations, that she demanded more than was fair, and nothing he did was ever good enough. He told a few stories that made the marriage situation definitely her fault. After about fifteen minutes, I began asking a different course of questions.

"Ted, how are you doing at fulfilling your God-given responsibility to Cindy?"

"I don't know," he said. "What do you mean?" So I opened my Bible and turned to Ephesians 5:25 and we read these words: *"Husbands, love your wives, just as Christ loved the church and gave himself up for her."* I let him look at the verse and then asked, "Ted, how are you giving up your life for Cindy?"

A strange look came over his face. "I don't know. I've never seen this before!"

I turned to 1 Peter 3:7 and we read the passage together. *"You husbands in the same way, live with your wives in an understanding way, as with someone weaker, since she is a woman; and show her honor as a fellow heir of the grace of life, so that your prayers will not be hindered" (NASB).*

Again I asked, "Ted, what do you do to honor your wife? Do you understand what is going on inside of her right now?" A little stunned, he answered the same way, "I don't know; I've never seen this before."

That meeting began a new direction for Ted and Cindy. I knew we could not fix their marriage until they got their priorities right. The three of us started meeting the next week to discuss how to have a Quiet Time, and they began to memorize verses together. After a few months, Cindy began to spend two hours each day alone with the Lord. Ted and I met one-on-one each week to talk about the above two passages, his responsibility as the head of the family, and his own walk with the Lord. I knew from experience that Ted was the key to getting his marriage back on track.

Ted began to change by doing special things for Cindy. He prayed for his wife daily, something he had never done before. Ted also realized that, growing up on a farm, he had observed that his dad came in from the fields and meals were always ready to eat. So Ted had developed a habit of coming home from work and demanding his food be ready. He often came through the door with the first thing out of his mouth being, "Where's my food?" or

"Hurry up, I'm hungry. Make me a sandwich." He remembered how his dad had said the exact same thing.

Like two ticks and no dog, this pattern of insisting their partner meet their needs was sucking the life out of both of them.

It had never occurred to Ted that this habit was dishonoring to his wife, or that she felt demeaned, unloved, and uncared for. Ted began to realize that the "relating patterns" he had picked up from his parents were killing his marriage. Just like his dad, Ted often treated Cindy in ways that made her feel unloved.

Cindy began to take her own struggles to the Lord in prayer. Over a period of time and with some outside help, she recognized the bitterness in her heart that came from her own shattered dreams and her unrealistic expectations for the marriage. She eventually admitted how she felt justified in venting that hurt at Ted.

As Ted and Cindy developed a love for the Lord, their ability to love each other improved. Over time, the marriage began to heal.

As their time alone with God deepened, they both discovered a new spiritual zeal to share Christ. Cindy led two women to Christ in her neighborhood, and Ted began to disciple a recent convert at their church. They still attended the weekly prayer meeting, but now they were praying with a new vision for their marriage, their children, and for opportunities to share Christ.

Their marriage struggled occasionally because old patterns die hard. But as they both made the Lord their focus and number one priority, their marriage changed dramatically. Ted and Cindy both recognized that only God could meet their individual needs. And demanding the other person make them feel wanted, loved, or special was a strategy that could never work.

Like two ticks and no dog, this pattern of insisting their partner meet their needs was sucking the life out of both of them. Instead, as they both went to God, His power, strength, and love gave them the ability to meet each other's needs according to God's plan. Over time, Ted and Cindy learned that God's design was a much better way!

Growing up on the farm, our hunting dog was constantly collecting ticks from the woods. Left alone, they would literally suck the life blood out of the dog. We constantly had to pull them off. Over the years, I've observed that some marriages are like that.

✓ What factors do you see as potential causes for a marriage breakup in the story about Ted and Cindy? Write down at least three observations about their marriage relationship. Be ready to discuss.

1.

2.

3.

The Impact of Culture and Media on Marriage

The biblical model of a man leading his marriage and family with the wife following his leadership is broken. Our culture and media have played a huge part in destroying these biblical roles for both men and women. On TV, most shows depict men as stupid and too inept to be leaders. Or they are portrayed as hormonally driven men whose only objective is to score another one-night stand with no consequences. Obviously, no woman in her right mind would trust such a man or want to follow his leadership.

Women are many times portrayed as only one-dimensional. They are sex trophies. They are shown to be both stupid and easy or the other extreme of being smart, but mean and controlling.

In our culture some women have become increasingly aggressive. Sometimes they compete with men as if there is a score to settle or a wound that drives them. They need to be in control, not allowing a man to ever hurt them again.

Some men have become more and more passive, not knowing how to lead because they have not seen good role models. Others feel bullied by their wives, and it is easier to follow than to confront the pattern.

In many marriages it is also normal that one or both are from divorced or single-parent homes. In some cases, the model of what a marriage should look like was filled with pain or there was no example at all.

God has given us a blueprint for a good and workable model of marriage. Each generation of Christians needs to discover what it is.

In any case, the biblical model has been broken. It has been turned upside down or is seen by some as old-fashioned or an out-of-touch relating pattern that won't work today.

Who's at fault here? Well, there's plenty of blame to go around. We have all grown up in a culture marred by sin. We have all been deeply wounded, and the lies we believed about love, sex, and what would bring us happiness have caused great heartache. Unfortunately, we bring this baggage into our marriages.

Hidden Agendas

Most men and women want to actually fall in love and have a long-term stable relationship. However, underneath the surface, we also have a hidden agenda: *We want the other person to meet our needs or take away our pain.* We want to feel loved unconditionally, accepted, and cared for. When the post-wedding exhilaration wears off, this secret objective comes to the forefront. When each is trying to get their needs met by "sucking the life out of the other," it's an endless battle, just like *"two ticks and no dog."*

Since this relating pattern can't work, couples begin to lash out at each other demanding, *"Meet my needs!"* Many times this is when the serious trouble starts.

We have very few models of godly, happy marriages. The default mechanism for how to do courtship or build a good marriage is mostly nonexistent. We've all been deeply scarred and the world has programmed us to have expectations that can only lead to disaster. *Is there any hope?*

Yes, there is hope! God has given us the blueprint for a good and workable model of marriage. Each generation of Christians needs to discover what it is.

✓ What role did the media have in shaping your view of love, courtship, and marriage? List at least two things.

1.

2.

✓ What effect did your parents' relationship have on you? Record an example or two.

✓ What hidden agendas did you bring into your marriage? (Hint: Your biggest marital disappointment will normally reveal your hidden agenda.)

✓ What hidden agenda do you feel your wife brought to the marriage?

THE MAN IS THE KEY

While the wife plays a significant role in the marriage relationship, I believe the man carries the greater responsibility. As men, we are the head, we are the ones God gives the role of leadership, and when we do not love or lead as God has designed, then we carry the larger responsibility for the failure.

But men, let's be honest. We are selfish! I have had dozens of discussions with men, just like Ted, who complained about their wives. I have never had a man tell me how excited he was to give up his life for her.

I've observed this in many marriages that were hurting. When the wife is struggling or deeply wounded, but the man walks with God and perseveres in loving his hurting wife, the chances of the marriage surviving go up dramatically. But when it's the man who is deeply struggling, even though his wife prays and goes to God with the issues, their chance of survival as a couple is much less. *The man is the key!* So men, let's figure out our God-given responsibility and fight for our marriages.

✓ *"The man carries a greater responsibility in the marriage."* Do you agree or disagree with this statement? Explain why or why not.

✓ What examples of selfishness have you observed in yourself or other men when it comes to the marriage relationship? Jot down at least two examples and be prepared to share.

Not Seeing Her Differences as a Gift from God

Over the years I've noticed two major mistakes that men make in marriage: 1. Not acknowledging his wife's differences as a gift from God, and 2. Embracing a wrong view of leadership. (We will discuss this second issue in our next lesson.)

Mistake number one is introduced in the first verse of the Bible on marriage, Genesis 2:18.

> ***The LORD God said, "It is not good for the man to be alone. I will make a helper suitable for him."***
>
> ***—Genesis 2:18***

✓ Why is it *"not good for the man to be alone?"* Jot down your thoughts.

When a married man grasps the truth of Genesis 2:18, that he is out of balance and his wife has been specifically designed by God to fill in the gaps of his personality, character, and thinking, then he has taken a huge step toward maturity.

God looked down and saw that Adam, the man, was incomplete. It was the man who needed something, not the woman. And it is true, when women stay single they still maintain the essence of how God has made them as a woman.

But generally when men are alone, either by never marrying or by divorce, something is missing. Many times (not always), personal growth comes to a stop. The lack of experience as a husband and father can leave some gaps in a man's development. God's plan is that most men should grow into the leaders, protectors, and providers he wants them to be in the context of marriage and family. And God has put these capabilities in every man.

Many men have big gaps when it comes to kindness, compassion, sensitivity, gentleness, and patience. These qualities are normally developed in the context of the relationship with our wife and children. If we do not allow these qualities to develop in our lives, we have the capacity to deeply hurt those closest to us, and many of us do.

What the Word "Helper" Means

Back in Genesis 2, God said that Adam needed a helper. This word *"helper,"* in the original language, is only used two ways in the Old Testament: It describes God as the *"helper"* of Israel and it expresses the *role of the wife* in her husband's life. It is a *highly exalted term* and, in the context of marriage, means *"one who fills up gaps."*

Men, God looks at you and sees holes, some wide gaps in who you are as a person. As men you and I are so out of balance that God saw we needed another person who is totally opposite and so different from us that only when we are together does it bring balance and harmony to what God wants created—a new unit called a *family.*

Not many twenty-year-old men are kind, sensitive, gentle, reliable, and not primarily focused on themselves. But a sixty-year-old man who has walked with God, loved his wife, and raised his children, develops the gentleness, understanding, insight, and wisdom that comes about as he gives up his life by focusing on his wife and children rather than himself.

When a man sees his wife's differences as a blessing, not as a threat to his manhood or a challenge to his leadership, he has grown. As men, we need to see our wives as the other side of a coin, with a perspective and set of gifts that, when brought together with our own, brings greater potential for what we can accomplish in life.

When a man sees his wife's perspective as wrong or invalid because it is different from his own and he refuses to consider its merit, he's an idiot! He is refusing to consider the advice of a person who has been specifically designed by the God of the universe to fill his gaps and cover his blind spots. *What a mistake!*

Never criticize your wife's judgment; look at whom she chose to marry!

This does not mean that your wife's opinion is the right one and yours is wrong. She may be just as out of balance as you are. But when we listen and consider those parts of her perspective that give balance to our own, we make better decisions and fewer mistakes.

Unfortunately, sometimes a marriage has so much pain that neither of the spouses can hear the other. When this happens, a couple may need professional help to get beyond the hurt and recommit to the roles that God has assigned to each of them. If this is you, don't despair. You have made it this far in the course, and you are laying the spiritual foundation for healing in your marriage. The man who walks with God and applies the three verses we will memorize on marriage, is giving his marriage the best chance of surviving.

After becoming a Christian, *marriage is the most life-changing event in a man's life.* When a man marries, he gives up his life in order to live for something larger than himself. He goes to work with a new zeal; he begins to think about permanence, buying a house, saving for the future, providing for his children. He comes to a whole new level of maturity as a man. *He just has fewer gaps!*

✓ *"When a married man grasps the truth of Genesis 2:18, that he is out of balance and his wife has been specifically designed by God to fill in the gaps of his personality, character, and thinking, then he has taken a huge step toward maturity."* Do you agree? Why or why not?

The LORD God said, "It is not good for the man to be alone. I will make a helper suitable for him."

—Genesis 2:18

Ask Questions

Is there:

A command to obey

A promise to claim

A sin to avoid

An application to make

Something new about God

Ask: Who, What, When, Where, Why

Emphasize:
Different words

Rewrite:
In your own words

✓ Do the *Ask Questions* method of meditation on Genesis 2:18 and record your thoughts.

✓ Now rewrite Genesis 2:18 in your own words.

✓ Before this study, what was your understanding of the word *"helper"* as it applied to your wife? How has it changed?

✓ What differences do you see in your wife that you know help to fill up gaps in you? List at least two.

✓ Spend some time praying, and ask God if there is anything that He wants to change in you as a husband. Jot it down.

✓ Review this lesson and organize your thoughts. Write down three or four key points that you want to remember. From now on you will write the *Points to Remember* each week. These lessons will have more reading. Use a highlighter or underline key parts to facilitate writing your own *Points to Remember.*

Points to Remember

1.

2.

3.

4.

Points that others shared that I want to remember:

Assignment for Next Week

1. Place Genesis 2:18 in the front pocket of your *EMAW Verse Pack* and memorize it this week. Start working on *My Marriage Commitment,* Ephesians 5:25, and 1 Peter 3:18 .

2. Spend extra time memorizing your verses on marriage. Spend at least one Quiet Time working on them. A friend of mine once said this about the verses he had memorized on marriage: "It was only after I had memorized the verses and said them one hundred times that they finally began to sink in, take root, and change me."

3. From now on we will have our Quiet Times on passages that apply to the topic we are studying. Have your Quiet Time in these passages this week: John 13:2-15; Matthew 20:20-28; John 12:23-28; and 1 Corinthians 13:1-13.

4. Begin praying daily for your wife and your growth into a godly husband.

✓ End in group prayer using the *WAR* method. Pray for your wives and marriages. Pray through any changes you need to make to be the husband God wants you to be.

Leader's Guide to

LESSON 2

THE GODLY HUSBAND

NOTE TO NEW LEADERS

You can download the Leader's Guide from the website *www.EveryManAWarrior.com* to make it easier to follow while leading the lesson. It is important to follow the Leader's Guide while leading the lesson. While some items are the same each week, others are special, one-time instructions that will negatively impact the study if missed.

THE GODLY HUSBAND

✓ Break into pairs and recite your verses to each other. Keep reciting the verses from Book 1 throughout the entire course.

✓ Sign off on the *Completion Record.*

✓ Open the session with prayer.

★✓ *Ask the men if they remembered to use the suggested passages for their Quiet Times.* Encourage them to use these passages to help them develop a greater understanding of the topic.

✓ Go around the room, asking each man to share one Quiet Time.

✓ Begin reading the lesson paragraph by paragraph.

✓ Pages 29–37: Ask each of the questions on these pages. Depending on time, have two to four people give their answer. Try to include everyone.

✓ Page 36: Have each man share his *Points To Remember.*

✓ Page 37: Read the *Assignment* together. Put Ephesians 5:25 and *My Marriage Commitment* in the front pocket of your *EMAW Verse Pack* and memorize them this week.

✓ End the group using the *WAR* method of prayer, praying for your wives and marriages. Pray through any changes you need to make to be the husband God wants you to be.

The Godly Husband

I was attending a couples' Bible study on the book of Genesis. We had gotten to the life of Jacob. Jacob had cheated his brother and fled to save his life. He then got a taste of his own medicine when his father-in-law deceived him and he ended up married to the wrong daughter! He did get the girl he wanted, but only by signing on as a servant for another seven years.

His two wives fought constantly, each competing for Jacob's love. Eventually, each wife gave a servant girl to Jacob so as to gain an advantage over the other sister in the procreation of children. As it was, there were now four women all fighting for Jacob's affections and his home was a war zone. To escape, Jacob often stayed away tending to the sheep.

During the Bible study discussion, one man named Stan made this comment, "I felt kind of sorry for Jacob. How would you live in a house where you had to try to control four women?" His wife, sitting across the circle, asked in a rather loud, perturbed tone of voice, "Control! What do you mean control?" The room went silent. The women were each glaring at their husbands, wondering if they felt the same way. The men were each looking at the floor, hoping that Stan would not get them all into trouble.

At the snack break later, the men gave their condolences to Stan, anticipating the ride home with his wife and what we all knew was coming. *Stan's view of leadership was about to be confronted.*

As Christian men, most of us need to be reprogrammed in our relational software if we are to make our own marriages work.

What Is Your Leadership Style and Where Did You Learn It?

As we discussed last week, all of us have a grid for what is normal in relationships. This default mode is being secretly developed inside the value center of every child as he or she is growing up. *"More is caught than taught"* is an old saying on raising children. Without even knowing it, we as children absorbed the attitudes, values, sense of right or wrong, and relating patterns from our parents and those around us. *How we treat our wives is greatly influenced by how we saw Dad treat Mom,* or how the predominant male in our life treated women.

When the pattern in our parents' marriage is good, we are blessed. But where there is anger, abuse, abandonment, alcohol, pornography, poor communication, divorce, and a whole list of other dysfunctions, we unknowingly bring a twisted model of "what's normal" into our own marriage.

For many men, our childhood experience is not a good model to reproduce. *As Christian men, most of us need to be reprogrammed in our relational software if we are to make our own marriages work.* Marriage confronts our selfishness, but when we put God's program to work, marriage is the sandpaper God uses to polish our character and lives.

✓ Who was the most influential male in your life (dad, uncle, grandfather, other)? How did he treat his wife or other women? Jot down your thoughts.

✓ Is the following statement true? Why? "Most of us need to be reprogrammed in our relational software if we are to make our own marriages work."

✓ How has marriage confronted your selfishness? List at least two examples of how God is using the sandpaper of marriage to polish you.

Wrong View of Leadership in the Home

Like Stan, above, most of us as men begin marriage with a wrong view of leadership in the home. There is nothing manly about being controlling, harsh, self-centered, insensitive, unsympathetic, unfeeling, unkind, demanding, critical, derogatory, or judgmental. *Jesus was none of these things and none of these attributes makes you a man.*

But Jesus was a perfect example of a real man! He had the courage to go to the Cross. He made a whip and drove out the moneychangers. He modeled gentleness in healing the sick and sensitivity in crying at the loss of Lazarus. He freely gave up His life, desires, and rights for the sake of others. He spent forty days fasting in the desert and at His weakest moment overcame Satan's greatest temptations. *Jesus was the perfect example of a real man. This is the model we should shoot for.*

Unknowingly, you teach your sons to disrespect their future wives and teach your daughters to be controlling because of the message they receive from you!

I cringe when I see a man come home and immediately complain or criticize something as insignificant as his dinner not being ready or the house being messy. *What are you doing?* I know what you are doing! I've done it myself. You're taking your frustration with life, your pain, or disappointment and dumping it on your wife. You bruise your relationship with your wife and life partner over something as insignificant as dirty dishes.

Unknowingly, you teach your son by your example t*o be disrespectful to his mother (and future wife),* and you teach your daughter to be controlling around men because the message they receive from you is "Men are selfish so watch out for yourself."

✓ Give an example of how you have taken your pain in life and dumped it on your wife.

✓ What message does this send to your children?

Hurt People Hurt People

Men, it is so easy take out our pain, insecurities, and woundedness on other people. That's why we need a deep and intimate walk with Christ. This habit of exploding our hurt on others is really a spiritual issue. It is true that hurt people end up hurting those closest to them.

We started this course by building your spiritual life. Our first memorized verses included Philippians 4:6-7. As we mature, we learn to take our pain and frustrations to the Lord, allowing Him to carry them rather than dumping them on others. Over time, God will do a healing work in our lives. If we do not have a growing relationship with God it becomes impossible to accomplish our job description as husbands: *to die to ourselves in order to live for something greater!* Instead, we pass our wounds and bad relationship programming onto our children.

The First Step for a Godly Husband Is Death to Self

For a man, dying to self so as to live for something bigger—his wife and children—is a hard but good thing. As we discussed last week, this dying process is part of coming to maturity as a man. It's the difference between ending up alone at the end of your life or enjoying deep and satisfying relationships.

Life is lived in the context of relationships, and when you die to those aspirations that are self-centered, your relationship with your wife and children can become one of the most fulfilling aspects of your life. When men don't die, they are unable to experience this truth.

✓ *"For a man, dying to self so as to live for something bigger—his wife and children—is a hard but good thing."* Is this statement true? Explain. Why is it a *good* thing?

✓ Jesus gave us a model of *"servant leadership."* Read John 13:3-15. Jot down your observations. What specific commands are given in verses 13-15?

✓ What are practical ways to demonstrate servant leadership to your wife? Jot down at least two possibilities.

Ask Questions

Is there:

A command to obey

A promise to claim

A sin to avoid

An application to make

Something new about God

Ask: Who, What, When, Where, Why

Emphasize:
Different words

Rewrite:
In your own words

What is your biblical job description as a husband?

✓ Use the *Ask Questions* method of meditating on Ephesians 5:25 and jot down your observations.

Husbands, love your wives, just as Christ loved the church and gave himself up for her.

—Ephesians 5:25

✓ What does the phrase *"gave himself up for her"* mean to you? What are some of the hardest things to *"give up"* for your wife? List at least two things.

✓ Rewrite Ephesians 5:25 in your own words and be prepared to share.

Your Marriage Can Be a Light in a Dark World

Observe how the character of a godly husband bore fruit in this next story.

Chuck, a missionary friend of mine, took his family to Brazil in 1960. They had a fruitful ministry and led many people to Christ. But his first convert taught him a valuable lesson.

Chuck had moved his family into a nice neighborhood and began to study the book of John with his neighbor Paulo. For months they studied the life and words of Jesus. Finally, Paulo received Christ as his Lord and Savior. Chuck was ecstatic, and after a few weeks Chuck was really itching to know what had been the key to this decision. So Chuck asked, "Paulo, was it our great Bible study time that brought you to Christ?" No! "Was it the illustration showing Christ as the bridge between God and man?" No! "Was it the great theological truths that I was able to explain?" No! "Then what was it?" Chuck asked, having exhausted his ideas.

Paulo told him this story. "About three months ago we were reading the Bible in your basement and your three young children were upstairs fighting. Your wife was trying to keep the kids in line, but after the third explosion she lost it and started yelling at the children. You excused yourself from our study and went upstairs to talk to your wife. *What brought me to Christ is what you did!* You went upstairs and took your overwhelmed, stressed-out wife in your arms and just held her. I was so stunned because I knew in my heart that my wife and I had never experienced that kind of relationship. I wanted what you and your wife had, and I knew Christ was the reason."

Our lives, our marriages, and our relationships with our children should be a bright light to those who are lost around us. Because a man who loves his wife like Christ loves His bride, the church, will stand out in our dark world where most people and marriages are hurting.

✓ How will changes in your marriage affect the people around you?

✓ What insight do you have into Chuck's relationship with his wife?

The Godly Husband

If you love your wife and give up your life for her,
If you show her honor and kindness on a regular basis,
If you learn to value her as a gift from God to give you balance and perspective,
If you do not resent her differences or be harsh with her as she struggles with her own woundedness,
If you give her grace as she wrestles to follow your leadership,
Then you are a man of God, a model to be imitated and a shining light in a dark world.
Your wife and children will honor you.

— by Lonnie Berger

✓ Which phrase from the above poem is most significant to you? Jot it down below and explain why.

✓ Write specific application to do this week to show your wife how much you value her.

To stimulate your thinking ask these questions:

Is there an apology to make?
Is there a gesture of love to show?
Are there some words that she longs to hear? Possible examples are: I love you! I cannot imagine my life without you! I'm so thankful for you! You complete me!
Is there a chore you can do that would lift her load?
Is there a gift to give?

This week I want to show my wife how much I value her by . . .

✓ Review the lesson and organize your thoughts. Jot down the most important *Points to Remember* from this lesson. Be prepared to share what you wrote.

Points to Remember

1.

2.

3.

4.

Points that others shared that I want to remember:

Assignment for Next Week

1. Have your Quiet Time in these passages this week: Colossians 3:1-14; Colossians 3:15-25; Ephesians 4:25-32; and Philippians 2:1-16.

2. ✓ Put Ephesians 5:25 and the *My Marriage Commitment* card in the front pocket of your *EMAW Verse Pack* and memorize them this week.

3. Memorize the *My Marriage Commitment* card just like a verse.

4. Be prepared to share with the group how your application *"to show value to your wife"* went.

✓ End the group using the *WAR* method of prayer. Pray through any changes you need to make to be the husband God wants you to be.

Memorize this card just like a verse.

My Marriage Commitment

It is my privilege to show my love for Jesus by caring for my wife—to love her, show her honor, try to understand her, and to give up my life and rights for her.

My Marriage Commitment

John 14:21; Ephesians 5:25; 1 Peter 3:7

Leader's Guide to

LESSON 3 WHEN MARRIAGES HURT

NOTE TO NEW LEADERS

You can download the Leader's Guide from the website *www.EveryManAWarrior.com* to make it easier to follow while leading the lesson. It is important to follow the Leader's Guide while leading the lesson. While some items are the same each week, others are special, one time instructions that will negatively impact the study if missed.

WHEN MARRIAGES HURT

✓ Break into pairs and recite all your verses and *My Marriage Commitment* to each other.

✓ Sign off on the *Completion Record.*

✓ Open the session with prayer.

★✓ Go around the room, asking each man to share one Quiet Time. Encourage the men to use the suggested passages to help them develop a greater understanding of the topic.

✓ Begin reading the lesson paragraph by paragraph.

✓ Pages 42-46: Ask each of the questions on these pages. Depending on time, have two to four people give their answer. Try to include everyone.

✓ Page 43: Have everyone read his summary rewrite of 1 Peter 4:19.

✓ Page 46: Have each man read his *Points to Remember.*

✓ Page 47: Read the *Assignment.* Have the men place 1 Peter 4:19 in the front pocket of their *EMAW Verse Pack.*

✓ Page 47: End the session practicing the *WAR* method of prayer. This may be a time when men want to pray about any hard issues confronting them in their marriages.

When Marriages Hurt

The ringing phone woke me out of a deep sleep at 11:45 p.m. It was Kevin, and he'd been drinking. With a slurred voice, he said, *"Lon, I'm going to do it! I'm tired of this crap; I'm going to leave my wife!"*

We'd had this conversation a number of times before. Perturbed and still a little groggy, I yelled into the phone, *"No, you're not! You are not going to hurt your four kids by leaving their mom! You are going to go to God and do what's right! Now go to bed and call me in the morning!"* He sheepishly said okay, and we hung up.

Kevin and Carol had come to Christ during college and had met in the church they both attended. They wanted to serve God even though neither had been raised in Christian homes. In their love for Christ, they defied all cultural norms of the 1970s and stayed sexually pure during their courtship.

But Kevin's anticipation of their honeymoon was shattered on their wedding night when Carol rolled up into the fetal position, pulled the covers over her head, and quietly sobbed. She later revealed that her older brother had sexually abused her during high school.

In the first decade of their marriage, sex was never good. Carol had performed her wifely duty even though Kevin knew she hated it and resented his physical needs. Now twenty years into their marriage, with four children, Kevin was losing hope. As they got into their late forties, Carol became increasingly angry toward him. Her bursts of rage and stares of hate were driving Kevin into depression and despair.

Now, they hardly ever had sex. Kevin's frustration kept mounting and once a month or so he would demand to have sex. Afterward, Carol would go sleep on the couch and seethe at him for days. Sex made her feel the horrors of her brother's abuse and caused her to explode at her husband.

Kevin was a gifted entrepreneur. His business had grown to be one of the most successful in the state. He worked 60 to 70 hours a week. At least at the office he felt successful, valued, and appreciated. Plus, it was an escape from the torture of home.

Kevin had never had an affair, although the temptation was high. He remembered his own shattered childhood when his dad had run away with his secretary, leaving Kevin's mom and three children. His dad had been a harsh, unloving man who constantly berated Kevin. Now with the potential collapse of his marriage, he again felt the bitterness and despair he remembered as a child.

Once when Kevin was struggling, he revealed to a close Christian brother the pain and hurt he was feeling. His friend rebuked him and said, "Toughen up! Stop your whining; lots of couples have sexless marriages."

Kevin and Carol began a rotation of seeing counselors, but no one was really helping. One Christian counselor told Kevin it was hopeless and he should file for a divorce. It was this counsel that brought Kevin to give me his late-night phone call. I told Kevin to come see me.

At our first meeting, I was not sure I would be able to help Kevin. But God was working in Kevin's heart. After our initial chit-chat, we prayed and I asked Kevin how I could help. His first statement gave me hope. With tears coming to his eyes he said, "Lonnie, during my drive over this afternoon, I prayed and told the Lord that I wanted Him to make me into the man He wanted me to be and that I would do whatever He told me in order to save my marriage!" Hearing this one statement of commitment, I decided I would do whatever I could to help Kevin.

Over the years I've thought many times about that phone call and the words God gave me. *"Go to God and do what's right!"* The phrase comes from 1 Peter 4:19. God had used the verse in my own life when He was taking me through my own time of marital testing.

> ***So then, those who suffer according to God's will should commit themselves to their faithful Creator [go to God] and continue to do good [what's right].***
>
> *—1 Peter 4:19 (emphasis added)*

(Some translations use "good"; others use "right." The Greek word means "a course of right action.")

In recent years this verse has become my definition for being a "real man of God." A real man of God responds to hurt, suffering, or trials by "going to God and doing what is right."

This does not mean that trials will be easy. God's plan is that trials will have a transforming effect on the kind of men we are. Sometimes the pain level necessary to change our character or values is quite high.

Kevin and Carol are still together even though the journey has been long and hard. They have found counselors who have helped them, and Kevin changed the way he relates to his wife on intimacy. Kevin's time with the Lord has deepened, and this hard-charging businessman has developed new levels of compassion and understanding that have transformed his relationship with both Carol and his children.

✓ Write three observations about Kevin's situation. How would you have responded if you had been Kevin?

So then, those who suffer according to God's will should commit themselves to their faithful Creator and continue to do good.

—1 Peter 4:19

Ask Questions

Is there:

A command to obey

A promise to claim

A sin to avoid

An application to make

Something new about God

Ask: Who, What, When, Where, Why

Emphasize:
Different words

Rewrite:
In your own words

Use the *Ask Questions* method of meditation on 1 Peter 4:19. Jot down your thoughts.

Use the *Emphasize Different Words* method. See Book 1, lesson 5, if you have forgotten how to use this method. What additional thoughts came to mind?

✓ Summarize the above two meditation exercises by rewriting 1 Peter 4:19 in your own words. Be prepared to share your rewrite with the group.

✓ Jot down a time when you went through something hard in your marriage. Were you able to go to God and do what's right? Why or why not?

✓ How did your response affect the situation? How would you respond to the same situation today?

✓ Read the three translations of Colossians 3:19 below. What commands are in these verses?

Husbands, love your wives and never treat them harshly. (NRSV)
Husbands, love your wives, and avoid any bitterness toward them. (NAB)
Husbands, love your wives and be gentle with them. (NCV)

—Colossians 3:19

✓ What happens to a woman's self-image when her husband is harsh, bitter, or not gentle?

✓ What happens in their marriage relationship when the husband is harsh, bitter, or not gentle?

✓ A godly husband is a man of godly character. Read 1 Peter 3:7-9. What character traits do you see in this passage?

✓ How does 1 Peter 3:9 apply to marriage? What happens in a marriage when a couple violates the command: *"Do not repay evil with evil or insult with insult . . . repay evil with blessing"?*

Marriage can be a place of great personal pain and suffering. Sometimes the desire to leave the marriage can be overwhelming, and many men do. However, I have observed over the years that some men who hang in there and let God teach them through the trials come out the other side being better men, more fulfilled in their marriages, and better fathers to their children.

Memo from God

My son,

When you are suffering, trust me. Trust me to do what's best for you. I measure things differently than you. I want what's best for your soul, what will give you spiritual rewards in heaven. Men measure what is easiest, what is free from pain, what gives them pleasure. I measure what will bring you the greatest joy, joy that will last, joy that is based on an eternal reward, joy that comes from knowing me.

God

✓ Read the *Memo from God* and record three to four observations on what God wants when you are going through hard times or suffering.

✓ From the memo, what do men want when they are suffering?

✓ Review the lesson. If your marriage is hurting, is it worth it to hang in there and do what's right even when we don't know the outcome? Why?

✓ Review the lesson and organize your thoughts. Jot down the most important *Points to Remember* from this lesson. Be prepared to share what you wrote.

Points to Remember

1.

2.

3.

4.

Points that others shared that I want to remember:

Assignment for Next Week

1. Have your Quiet Times in the following passages: Isaiah 61:1-3; Luke 4:16-21; 2 Corinthians 1:1-11; Galatians 6:1-9; John 8:1-11. As you meditate, these passages will help you grasp some key biblical principles for the next lesson.

2. ✓ Place 1 Peter 4:19 in the front pocket of your *EMAW Verse Pack* and memorize it this week.

✓ End the session practicing the *WAR* method of prayer. This may be a time when men want to pray about any hard issues confronting them in their marriages.

Note from the author: **I understand that not every marriage can be saved. In the next lesson we will discuss some of the realities of how woundedness can impact a marriage.**

Leader's Guide to

LESSON 4 THE WOUNDED WIFE

NOTE TO NEW LEADERS

You can download the Leader's Guide from the website *www.EveryManAWarrior.com* to make it easier to follow while leading the lesson. It is important to follow the Leader's Guide while leading the lesson. While some items are the same each week, others are special, one-time instructions that will negatively impact the study if missed.

THE WOUNDED WIFE

✓ Break into pairs and recite all your verses to each other.

✓ Sign off on the *Completion Record.*

✓ Ask someone to open the session with prayer.

✓ Go around the room, asking each man to share one Quiet Time.

✓ Begin reading the lesson paragraph by paragraph.

✓ Pages 52-59: Ask each of the questions on these pages. Depending on time, have two to four people give their answer. Try to include everyone.

✓ Page 60: Have each man share his *Points to Remember.*

✓ Page 61: Read the *Assignment* together. Put 1 Peter 3:7 in the front pocket of your *EMAW Verse Pack* and memorize it this week.

✓ End in prayer using the *WAR* method. Pray for your wife and marriage. Pray through any changes you need to make to be the husband God wants you to be.

THE WOUNDED WIFE

Janice was an only child. Growing up, many times she felt a sense of loneliness. Her parents had a hard time conceiving, and it seemed almost a miracle that she was born. Having tried unsuccessfully for a number of years, they were in their late thirties when she finally arrived. Janice's mom was outgoing and loved people. However, her dad was the opposite. He was a nonemotional, sometimes harsh man who never showed affection, gave verbal affirmation, or hugs to his little girl. Janice could not remember him ever saying *"I love you"* or that she was special.

In high school Janice was deeply insecure about her looks, although she was quite attractive. As a sophomore she had her first boyfriend, a senior named Patrick. She felt a sense of love and contentment in his arms that she had never known before. When she was with him all her loneliness evaporated. He was her first love and her initiation into sex. Once they started having sex, they seemed to have no control. This went on for eight months until Patrick went to college in another state.

At first he called regularly, but then he broke it off, and Janice found out that he was seeing someone else. She felt angry, used, discarded, and depressed. She began to wonder if their relationship had really been about love. Would Patrick have still pursued her if she had not given him sex?

Janice felt she had lost something very precious, but she wasn't sure what it was. In the midst of her pain she longed to feel that special sense of being loved and wanted. Her dad noticed her sadness but said nothing. Within a few weeks a boy she had always liked asked her out. The excitement and thrill of being pursued was like an overpowering drug. On their second date she gave herself away again.

Throughout high school and into college, a pattern developed. She gave herself to feel loved—and sex was always the currency of exchange. When the thrill of being wooed wore thin, Janice would break off the relationship. Being pursued and the thrill of a new love were addicting.

This pattern continued into her junior year of college when she began to want something more permanent. When the guy she was dating fled, a sense of deep sadness and emptiness overwhelmed her. She felt like she had given a tiny bit of her heart to each relationship—and now there was nothing left. Even the adrenaline rush of being pursued no longer filled the void in her heart.

The excitement and thrill of being pursued was like an overpowering drug.

In her junior year of college, Janice met Kathy, who invited her to come to a Bible study. Her parents had attended church on Christmas and Easter, but Janice knew little about the Bible, so she accepted. Within a few months Janice gave her heart to Christ. For the first time in her life she felt a new kind of love. She first felt it from the girls in her Bible study. As she grew in spending time with Jesus, she sensed God's love, acceptance, and forgiveness.

During her senior year she met Ken at a Christian conference. Their eyes met and almost instantly they fell in love. They were married six months later, right after graduation.

During the next ten years Ken and Janice had two children and were deeply involved in their church. They attended a couples' Bible study, Ken ushered, and Janice taught Sunday school. As soon as their two children were in school, Janice went back to work. Ken had a good job, but with their growing family they needed a bigger house.

She had developed a coping mechanism of giving herself to men as a way of deadening the pain.

Unknown to Ken, Janice was struggling. She loved her husband, and they had sex on a regular basis. But something else, deep inside, was driving her. Janice longed for the excitement and thrill of new love. This driving force grew until she found herself having an affair with a coworker. It only lasted a few weeks, but Janice felt so guilty that she told Ken. They went to see their pastor and he counseled with them. Ken was hurt deeply but said he was able to forgive her and they could move on.

Two years later, Janice had another affair with a different coworker. This time Ken was furious but not sure what he should do. It was at this point I got a call from him.

Ken and Janice are still together. Their two children are both married and have children of their own. Janice had three years of counseling—which led to her discovery of the deep wound caused by her emotionally absent father. She had developed a coping mechanism of giving herself to men as a way of deadening the pain. Even her affairs were not really about sex, Ken, or their marriage, but about her need to feel wanted, pursued, and valued.

It took Ken a long time before he could trust Janice again. He had his own spiritual journey and lessons God wanted to teach him. It took time, but Ken finally began to understand the woundedness of his wife. Before her affairs, they had sex on a regular basis—so he thought the relationship was fine. He had not realized Janice's deep longing to feel valued and cherished. She wanted to feel loved, just for who she was, not for her ability to give sex to a man. Otherwise, sex was too much like her previous relationships, in which she had always felt devalued and left empty.

✓ Write down three observations you have about the story above.

✓ What role did Janice's father have in her promiscuity?

✓ What should Ken have done when Janice had her first affair? Her second affair?

✓ Why do you think Ken did not see Janice was struggling?

WOUNDEDNESS BROUGHT TO MARRIAGE

Woundedness is a relative term. Some people, both men and women, have been so deeply wounded during their childhoods that they spend their whole lives trying to compensate. Others, by the grace of God, were raised in homes where they found nurturing, care, love, and verbal messages that were uplifting.

So . . . I'm mostly your fault!

But Happy Birthday anyway!

Your daughter

Most of us are somewhere in between.

Every wounded wife was once a little girl and her father had a huge influence in her life. A girl develops her sense of value, worth, and self-esteem from her dad. Every little girl first learns to practice her femininity on her father. If you have raised a daughter, then you know the special bond that forms between a daddy and his little girl.

For a woman, the relationship she has with her dad—the first man in her life—creates a homing device that will determine the men she relates to and how she interprets what love is. This does not mean that we, men or women, can pass off responsibility for our poor choices to our fathers. While a father may leave a deep hole in our life, we each choose how to fill it.

As we discussed in Lesson 1, cultural factors have a huge influence as this little girl grows into a woman. Unfortunately, the cultural brainwashing she receives can be immensely destructive.

Somewhere in our nation's history, men have lost the will to protect their daughters' sexual purity. Now female sexuality is exploited for corporate profits, and we are all the poorer for it.

When a man brings his own woundedness into the marriage relationship, combining it with his wounded wife, the potential for a failed marriage is high.

But right into the middle of this volcano of pain ready to explode, Jesus steps in. Into the mess we have made of our own lives, He comes without condemnation, but with grace, love, and the power to heal. Obviously this may take some time, perhaps even years.

Once again, the man is the key. Because inside every wounded wife is a little girl who longs to be loved and cherished. If she did not feel it from her dad, then the need to be assured of your love is even more intense.

Many men wrestle with what seems so unfair: having their dreams in marriage shattered by their wife's hidden pain. Some men have subconsciously hoped that marriage would be a place where their own hurt would be taken away—only to discover that their wife is also deeply wounded. (Again two ticks and no dog.)

Even if your wife is deeply wounded and unable to fulfill her role as a biblical wife, that does not give you a free card to disobey God. *You are still commanded to love her, to cherish her, and give up your life for her.* Yes, it may be unfair. But Jesus understands unjust suffering. He has promised eternal rewards for your obedience, especially in hard or unusual circumstances. *If you do not care for your wounded wife, who will?*

> ***For it is commendable if a man bears up under the pain of unjust suffering because he is conscious of God. But how is it to your credit if you receive a beating for doing wrong and endure it? But if you suffer for doing good and you endure it, this is commendable before God. To this you were called, because Christ suffered for you, leaving you an example that you should follow in his steps. "He committed no sin, and no deceit was found in his mouth." When they hurled their insults at him, he did not retaliate; when he suffered, he made no threats. Instead, he entrusted himself to him who judges justly.***
>
> *—1 Peter 2:19-23*

Jesus understands the pain of unjust suffering. There is never hopelessness when Jesus is our focus, even though sometimes we may lose hope! His grace is always there for you, and it is only through Christ that healing can happen.

✓ What thoughts do you have about Jesus' ability to heal a hurting marriage?

✓ How would you counsel a brother in Christ whose marriage is deeply hurting because of a wounded wife and his dreams of a wonderful marriage are being shattered? (If nothing comes to mind, review Lesson 3.)

✓ What do you think of the following statement? "Even if your wife is deeply wounded and unable to fulfill her role as a biblical wife, it does not give you a free card to disobey God. You are still commanded to love her, to cherish her, and give up your life for her." Explain your thoughts and be prepared to share.

In Lesson 2 we focused on the command in Ephesians 5:25 for husbands to *give up their life* for their wives. This week we will focus on another key issue: Understanding them!

I know many men feel that understanding their wife is asking the impossible. *Men Are from Mars, Women Are from Venus,* by John Gray, has sold millions of copies. But God did not set us up for failure in giving us this command. When God gave us 1 Peter 3:7, He had something very specific in mind: *your growth as a man.*

You husbands in the same way, live with your wives in an understanding way, as with someone weaker, since she is a woman; and show her honor as a fellow heir of the grace of life, so that your prayers will not be hindered.

—1 Peter 3:7 NASB

✓ Meditate on these key phrases from 1 Peter 3:7 using the *Emphasize Different Words* method. What do they mean? How will you apply them?

	What They Mean	***How I Will Apply Them***
Live with your wives		
Understanding way		
Show her honor		
Prayers may not be hindered		

✓ Rewrite 1 Peter 3:7 in your own words. Be prepared to share.

✓ How will understanding your wife affect your marriage? How will it change you?

A Special Gift in Marriage

God has given every man a special gift in marriage. Because inside every woman is a God-given longing to feel valued by her husband. The Greek word that is translated *"honor"* in 1 Peter 3:7 could also be translated as *"precious."* Your wife longs to feel *valued, prized, loved, treasured, needed, and precious.* And she longs for these messages to come from you.

Men, do you want to become the man God wants you to be? Then treat your wife in the way God commands. Learn specific ways that communicate how precious your wife is to you. *Make it your God-given job description to speak or do at least one of these each week.*

✓ Jot down three things that you can do to make your wife feel loved, cherished, and precious.

1.

2.

3.

Possible Applications

Tell her "I love you," every day.
Bring her flowers for no reason at all.
Vacuum the house, just because it needs it.
Do the dishes or clean the bathroom as an "I love you "gift.
Learn to give her "nonsexual" touching.
Figure out what her love language is and do it often![1]

1 Gary Chapman, *The 5 Love Languages* (Chicago, IL: Northfield, 2010)

✓ Which one will you do this week?

Sometimes our wives are so wounded that they cannot feel our love even when we work hard at sending the message. The conflicts that result may need some professional help. Below are some principles of dealing with conflicts caused by deeper woundedness.

Dealing with Conflict in a Hurting Marriage

The first step in dealing with the conflict that happens in hurting marriages is to define the root source of the conflict.

People carry some deep hurts. The wound is like a festering volcano of pain just waiting for the stimuli to explode. This pain can detonate whenever the wound is touched by a similar event that subconsciously triggers an emotional outburst far worse than the issue that triggers the response.

When an emotional explosion erupts, people do not tend to connect the present-day event to the underlying wound that happened years ago. It makes more logical sense to blame a present-day person than to accept the pain they feel as an historical echo of the original wound.

How to Respond:

1. Reframe the conflict. See the conflict as a trigger that connects your spouse to her woundedness.
2. See your partner's hurtful behavior as an overflow of her woundedness. Remember she did not have control over her childhood. She did not ask to be abandoned, abused, rejected, or shamed.
3. Release each other from the lie that your spouse is responsible for your

present joy or unhappiness. True joy can only be found in Christ and being in His will for our lives.

4. Abandon the misguided strategy to change your partner so as to make you happy. These attempts are rooted in the lie of number 3 above.

5. Work at making the connection between today's conflicts and your own personal woundedness. It is easy to wrongly assume that your current pain is due to present relationships. This is rarely the case in deeply rooted relationship conflicts.

6. Find a competent counselor or resource to help you focus on your own healing, rather than staying in bondage to the lie that your pain is your partner's responsibility. Some groups actually hinder the healing process because they keep the focus on blaming the partner.[2]

(Special Note: This lesson is designed for men who find themselves married to a deeply wounded wife. However, in some marriages the husband is also deeply wounded or the more wounded of the two. These principles work both ways.)

✓ What observations do you have from these points about responding to conflict? What do you agree or disagree with? Be prepared to share.

✓ Review the lesson and organize your thoughts. Jot down the most important *Points to Remember* from this lesson on page 60. Be prepared to share what you wrote.

2 Ed M. Smith, Beyond Tolerable Recovery (Alathia, 2000).

Points to Remember

1.

2.

3.

4.

Points that others shared that I want to remember:

Assignment for Next Week

1. ✓ Put 1 Peter 3:7 in the front pocket of your *EMAW Verse Pack* and memorize it this week.

2. Next week we start on the topic of raising children. Have your Quiet Times in the book of Proverbs. Chapters 2, 3, 4, 5, 6, and 7 all start with, "My son . . ." Read any of these chapters and begin thinking about principles for raising children.

3. The coming lessons require more reading. Use a highlighter or underline key parts to facilitate writing your own *Points to Remember*.

✓ End the session practicing the *WAR* method of prayer. This may be a time when men want to pray about any hard issues confronting them in their marriages.

Special Note
We have only spent a few weeks on the topic of marriage and there is much that we could not cover. If possible, attend a Christian marriage conference or purchase some of the excellent material on marriage you can find at your local Christian bookstore. *Like becoming a better man, improving your marriage is a lifelong process. But it is always worth the investment!*

LESSONS 5-8 RAISING CHILDREN

SPECIAL NOTE

Lessons 5–8 are long. Depending on your group size and the time that you have allotted, you may want to take two weeks on each lesson. A suggested breaking point is given in each lesson.

If you do break the lessons into two weeks, make the following adjustments:

1. Continue to review verses and share Quiet Times each week. Use this slower pace to get your verses fully memorized.

2. After Lesson 5 you will have an additional assignment to spend one hour a week with one of your children or grandchildren.

3. Each week you will report back to the group what you did with your child using the father-daughter, father-son principles learned in Lesson 5.

4. In preparation for the second week, try to reread the whole lesson. Many men did not have a good parenting model growing up. Rereading the stories and thinking about the lesson questions will help you grasp this material at a deeper level.

5. Put the next verse in the front pocket of your *EMAW Verse Pack* and start memorizing it.

6. End the lesson using the *WAR* method of prayer.

7. *It is important to follow the Leader's Guide while leading the lesson. While some items are the same each week, others are special, one-time instructions that will negatively impact the study if missed. They are marked with a star.* ★

Leader's Guide to

LESSON 5

Turning the Hearts of Fathers to Their Children

Note to New Leaders

You can download the Leader's Guide from the website *www.EveryManAWarrior.com* to make it easier to follow while leading the lesson.

Turning the Hearts of Fathers to Their Children

✓ Break into pairs and recite all your verses to each other.

★✓ Count the number of recorded Quiet Times you have in the back of the book. You should have ten or more. Sign off on the *Completion Record.*

✓ Ask someone to open the session with prayer.

★✓ Read the special note on the previous page. Decide as a group if you want to take two weeks on these lessons.

✓ Go around the room asking each man to share one Quiet Time.

✓ Begin reading the lesson paragraph by paragraph.

✓ Pages 65-77: Ask each of the questions on these pages. Depending on time have two to four people give their answer. Try to include everyone.

✓ Page 69: Have each person read their summary on training children from God's perspective in the Greek word *paideuo.*

★✓ Page 71: *Break lesson here.* Place the *Three Biblical Principles on Raising Children* in the front window of your *EMAW Verse Pack* and start memorizing it this week. Remember to review verses and share Quiet Times at the beginning of the second week.

✓ Page 77: Have each person read their *Points to Remember.*
✓ Page 78: Read the *Assignment.*
✓ Page 78: Plan a one-hour outing with one of your children or grandchildren and be prepared to report back to the group.
✓ Page 78: Remind them to use a highlighter or underline in the lesson to help with writing their own *Points to Remember.*
✓ End in group prayer using the *WAR* method. Spend some time praying for your children.

Turning the Hearts of Fathers to Their Children

EVERY MAN A WARRIOR

Scott had owned a construction company. During the 1950s through the 1980s, he built hundreds of homes all over Omaha. We were new to the city and looking for a place to live. We ended up renting one of his properties.

As a teenager on the farm I had learned wiring and electricity. I had also worked my way through college doing construction and building houses. Scott, now retired and in his seventies, needed help from time to time on some of his properties. An electrical job in a basement remodel brought us together.

As he was watching me pull some wire through the conduit he began to talk. He was financially well off and we had often discussed his investments and the stock market. But he had not been successful with his children. Now older, he was looking back at his life. With considerable pain, he blurted out these words, "My son is an idiot. He should be over here helping me do this, but he doesn't know how to do anything. He can't even hang drywall and %$#&*! I don't have the time to teach him."

When Scott died a few years later, his son did not even come to his dad's funeral.

Three Biblical Principles on Raising Children

The above story is very sad, but true. This story exemplifies three of the most significant truths I've learned in raising children during the past few decades.

We will memorize these principles this week and apply them throughout our study. These principles are taken from the Scripture and I believe they are essential for you to become the dad God wants you to be.

Three Biblical Principles on Raising Children:

- *It is the father's God-given responsibility to train his children.*

  (Ephesians 6:4)

- *Children get their self-image from what they believe Dad thinks about them.*

  (Proverbs 17:6)

- *The words spoken to a child will determine his or her destiny.*

  (Proverbs 18:21)

Fathers, do not exasperate your children; instead, bring them up in the training and instruction of the Lord.

—Ephesians 6:4

And the glory of children are their fathers.

—Proverbs 17:6, KJV

The tongue has the power of life and death.

—Proverbs 18:21

✓ Review the *Three Biblical Principles on Raising Children.* Jot down one example (good or bad), from your childhood or in raising your own children that relates to each of these principles.

It is the father's God-given responsibility to train his children.

(Ephesians 6:4)

Children get their self-image from what they believe Dad thinks about them.

(Proverbs 17:6)

The words spoken to a child will determine his or her destiny.

(Proverbs 18:21)

Discovering Your God-Given Role as a Dad

Fred had four children. The two eldest teenagers were partying, sleeping around, and smoking pot. His wife wanted Fred to talk to me. Fred described all the bad decisions that his kids were making, and after an hour of listening and grieving with Fred, I asked him this question: "Fred, what do you think your biblical role is as a father to your children?" His answer was very revealing.

"My role as a father!" he shot back. "I'm just a paycheck! I bring the money home, give it to my wife, and she takes care of the children." When I suggested that this concept might be a part of the problem, Fred became angry. "Well, I'm doing a much better job raising my children than my dad did with me!"

Unfortunately, this statement was true. On a scale of 1 to 100 his dad was a minus 500. Fred's childhood had been awful; his dad had been brutal. But Fred had come to Christ—and knew he was to be completely different in his parenting methods than his father was. In truth, he had moved 500 points away from his dad's horrible example. But now the pendulum had just swung to zero. *He needed to discover God's standard for being a father.* We began to meet each week.

Over the years I've had a number of men voice the same statement to me: *"I'm doing a lot better job than my dad did with me."* But as Christian men, we need to discover God's standard—and not use our dad's parenting example—as the measuring stick or an excuse.

My friend Joe was attending a men's camping retreat with some of his church friends. They were all in their early fifties and each had recently lost his dad. Sitting around the campfire, one of the men asked Joe, "Do you miss him much?" Joe replied, "Well, not really. We did not have a close relationship." Joe threw out the question to the whole group: "Do you miss your dads?" Each man had virtually the same story. There was not much to miss, since none of the men had felt close to their fathers. Tragically, this is the norm for many men.

In the last verse of the Old Testament, God says that one of His purposes for sending the Messiah is that *"He will turn the hearts of fathers to their children"* (Malachi 4:6). A child who does not have a close relationship with his or her dad is one of the great tragedies of living in a fallen world. But God's plan is always redemption, the buying back of something lost or stolen. For every father who comes to Christ, God's plan is to turn that man's heart back to his children.

To do that, we need to be reprogrammed. You and I will parent our children the same way we were parented unless we get a biblical upgrade on parenting. Like Scott, Fred, and Joe, we need to rethink and discover anew our biblical role and responsibility in being the fathers God wants us to be.

Fathers, do not exasperate your children; instead, bring them up in the training and instruction of the Lord.

—Ephesians 6:4

In Ephesians 6:4, God gives us, as fathers, the responsibility for the training of our children. If we do not do it, the world will. God wants to help us succeed as dads. So He put inside the heart of every child a deep, deep longing for his or her father's approval. Children get their self-image from what they believe Dad thinks about them. *It's in their God-given design.* If we as dads don't learn how to train our children, then we set them up for failure and, in some cases, a life of misery.

✓ Describe your relationship with your dad. How did he train you?

✓ Jot down two things that you want to imitate from your dad's life and parenting style. Then jot down two things that you want to do differently with your children.

Imitate Dad	*Don't Imitate Dad*
1.	*1.*
2.	*2.*

Some Christians seem to only know one verse on raising children—*"spare the rod and spoil the child."* Actually, that's not a quote from the Bible but a misleading commentary on Proverbs 13:24. The verse is actually an admonition for fathers to love their children enough to give careful thought to their training.

This week you should have at least one Quiet Time in Hebrews 12:1-11, a key passage on how God disciplines His children. The Greek word used in Hebrews 12 for discipline is *paideuo.* It is a synonym for the word *"instruction"* in Ephesians 6:4. Unfortunately, we do not have an accurate corresponding word in the English language, so *paideuo* is translated into discipline or chastisement. The meaning is far broader than that.

***Paideuo* (used in Hebrews 12 on how God trains His children):**

Speaks to the raising and education of children.
Speaks to the thoughts and attitudes of the heart and encourages a child to have proper boundaries.
Speaks to instruction of or the building of wisdom into a child.
Speaks to the training and development of a child by setting an example for them to follow.
Speaks to rewarding a child for good behavior and punishment for bad.
The discipline of God is meant to shape you.

He who spares the rod hates his son, but he who loves him is careful to discipline him.

—Proverbs 13:24

✓ Review the list above. Write a paragraph summary about training children from the thoughts and definitions given above on the Greek word *paideuo.*

While corporal punishment is a part of rearing children, it is not the central theme of what the Bible teaches. Shaping a child's character is the most significant aspect taught in the Scripture with regard to raising children.

The words *training* and *instruction* are almost identical in the English language. In the Greek, the word *training* can be translated as *"nurture"* and has to do with the *"molding of character."* The King James Version uses the word *nurture* in its translation.

Fathers, do not exasperate your children; instead, bring them up in the training and instruction of the Lord.

—Ephesians 6:4

Ask Questions

Is there:

A command to obey

A promise to claim

A sin to avoid

An application to make

Something new about God

Ask: Who, What, When, Where, Why

Emphasize:
Different words

Rewrite:
In your own words

✓ Do the *Ask Questions* method of meditation on Ephesians 6:4. Jot down your thoughts.

✓ Look up the word *exasperate* in a dictionary or thesaurus. What does it mean? Give an example of how a father might exasperate his children.

✓ Now rewrite Ephesians 6:4 in your own words. Be prepared to share.

Some of us had no father or our father was a bad example. If this is you, *I've got good news.* These four lessons will begin your training to become an excellent dad. Read and reread these lessons until they have soaked into your heart. They can give you a new and biblical model for being a father to your children.

Shaping a child's character is the most significant aspect of parenting taught in the Scripture.

★ **Break here if you are spending two weeks on the lesson.**

Learning to Build into Our Children

Years ago, when my two children were small, God changed my life forever in how I looked at raising children. I was leading a financial-planning seminar in Des Moines, Iowa, along with my boss and good friend, Scott. He asked if we could adjust the schedule. His grown daughter, who was working in Minneapolis, was driving down to see him. I said, Sure, no problem.

It takes wisdom to have a good family, and it takes understanding to make it strong. It takes knowledge to fill a home with [children that are*] rare and beautiful treasures.

—Proverbs 24:3-4, NCV (added by the author)*

After Scott got back, I asked how his time went. "Great," he replied. "Was your daughter down here for work?" I asked."No." "Did she have another reason for being here?" "No, just to see me for lunch," he replied. ***What?*** I was more than curious. I asked for clarification, "Your daughter drove five hours one way from Minneapolis and now is driving back five hours to Minneapolis, just to see you for a two-hour lunch?" The next words out of his mouth left me flabbergasted. "Yes, she did. After my wife, my daughter is one of my best friends!"

That was the first time I had ever heard someone speak such a thought. It was a totally new concept to me. It left me puzzled since I did not know or think such a relationship between a father and a child was possible. That five-minute conversation changed my life. I went home from that meeting asking God to teach me how to build such a relationship with my own children.

How to Have a Successful Father-Daughter or Father-Son Time

Building into the lives of our children means spending one-on-one time with them. I have two children, both girls. We call it father-daughter time. If you have sons you will get to do a lot more rough-and-tumble stuff than I did. But the time talking and just being together is where most of the training happens.

We started father-daughter time when my kids were three and five. At first it was just a Happy Meal at McDonald's. Even at that age, their self-image was developing. Time alone, talking with Dad, may be the most significant self-image-builder there is.

When the teenage years hit, time alone with Dad was a deeply ingrained relational pattern. If we had not established the habit early, it would have been harder to start.

However, I have witnessed some amazing relational turn-around experiences between men and their children. When a dad figures out what God wants for him as a father, and he pursues his children, they will respond. Trust may have to be rebuilt, and it will take some time. But with God's help relationships can be restored. Rebuilding wounded relationships with our children will be the topic in Lesson 8.

This Is a Process—You Will Change Too!

You will need time to develop into a dad that your children can and want to talk to. You are on a learning curve as well. If your dad did not spend one-on-one time with you, then learning how to talk to your children at a deeper level will take some time. But it will pay big dividends later.

I'm not saying every man should be best friends with his children. But I am saying that most of us can definitely have a better relationship with our children than our dads had with us. The level of closeness that a child has with his or her father greatly impacts their self-image—and eventually their own relationship with God.

Think about one of your children. What is one way you could spend time with him or her to talk? This does not have to be a long stretch of time. Most of my father-daughter times were at the local Burger King. Many times out of a whole hour we did not have any deep spiritual or intellectual discussion. Other times there might be only five minutes or less on a deeper topic. Don't be discouraged. ***That's normal!***

And the glory of children are their fathers.

—Proverbs 17:6 KJV

The key here is that you choose to spend time with them. You choose to ask them questions. The message is clear to the child: *You value them highly and want to spend time with them.* Spending time with dad can make the heart of a child light up!

A friend of mine is a medical doctor and works lots of hours. We met to talk about his concerns for his children. Some things were not going well, so we discussed what the problem might be. That next Saturday he canceled his golf time with his friends and spent two hours playing basketball in the driveway with his kids, ages twelve, fourteen, and sixteen. Later that weekend, independent of each other, they each said these words, "Dad, thanks for playing ball with us."

When he told me this story a week later, he had tears in his eyes. He finally got it! His absence was sending a clear message to his kids: "You're not valuable enough for me to spend time with you!" He has set aside golf for now because he sees he only has a few years left with these three children.

✓ Review the three *Biblical Principles on Raising Children* and answer the following. What does it say to the heart of a child when you spend one-on-one time with him or her? How does it affect a child when he or she is ignored? Why?

Time-Tested Principles for a Successful Father-Daughter or Father-Son Time

Make it safe. *The child has to know that he or she can share anything and you will not criticize or be angry.*

Learn to ask questions. *You cannot build into your son or daughter unless you know what's going on inside that child. I normally started with such simple questions as, "Tell me about you!" or "How's it going at ________________?" (school, sports, certain classes, certain relationships, or whatever is going on in their life you should know about).*

Make it mostly about them. *Your actions speak louder than words. If you do most of the talking, it's a bust. But whenever you spend one-on-one time with your children and keep the focus on them, it communicates tremendous value to them. It communicates love in a way they desperately long for.*

Shut up and listen. *"For out of the overflow of the heart the mouth speaks!" (Matthew 12:34b). It is when your child is talking that you can discover what he or she is excited about, facing, struggling with, or hurting from. (This leads to the next point.)*

Pray with them. *After every father-daughter time, about a block from home I would grab my daughter's little hand and I prayed over what we had talked about. The prayer was short and just about them. They never turn down prayer when they are the focus. Plus you get to model Philippians 4:6-7, talking to God about everything we face in life.*

Speak a "building block of truth" into their lives. *We will discuss this in-depth next week.*

✓ Review Page 74. Which of these principles do you want to implement more fully in raising your children? List at least two and jot down why.

✓ Assignment for next week: Plan a one-hour outing with one of your children or grandchildren. Measure your time with them against these five criteria. Be prepared to report to the group.

Did you:
Make it safe?
Ask questions?
Keep the focus on them?
Listen?
Pray over them?

Give yourself a score of: ____________

5—I did well.
3—I'm still learning.
1—I have a lot of work to do.

My Favorite Passage on Father-Daughter, Father-Son Time

✓ Spend some time meditating on Deuteronomy 6:5-7, on the next page. Jot down your thoughts.

> ***Love the LORD your God with all your heart and with all your soul and with all your strength.***
> ***These commandments that I give you today are to be upon your hearts. Impress them on your children. Talk about them when you sit at home and when you walk along the road, when you lie down and when you get up.***
>
> *—Deuteronomy 6:5-7*

✓ When you consider this passage, how important is open communication between you and your children?

✓ What happens to your ability to influence your children when communication stops? Explain why.

✓ What impact does your time in the Word have on your ability to pass truth to your children?

Deuteronomy 6:5-7 is my favorite passage on the role of one-on-one time with a son or daughter. *The key to being able to impress our children with biblical values is that the truth has first touched your heart.* It is only when the truth of the Scripture has embedded itself in our lives that it is readily available to pass on to our children. Most opportunities to pass our values to our children happen in the normal day-to-day activities of life—when you sit at home watching a movie, when you are at the breakfast table on a Saturday, or when you take a walk together just to find out what is going on in their lives.

Some parents seem to make their Christianity about rules, and they want their kids to follow those rules to the letter. But God starts this passage with relationship. Love me! God sees this command as the starting point and most important truth to pass on to our children about being a Christian. Tell your sons and daughters to love God! Model it. Share with them often about your walk with the Lord and what He is teaching you. Children are most effectively taught when they first observe in us the biblical truths we are trying to teach them.

✓ Review the lesson, organize your thoughts, and jot down the most important *Points to Remember* from this lesson. Be prepared to share what you wrote.

Points to Remember

1.

2.

3.

4.

Points that others shared that I want to remember:

Assignment for Next Week

1. ✓ Place the *Three Biblical Principles on Raising Children* in the front pocket of your *EMAW Verse Pack* and memorize it this week.

2. Have your next one or two Quiet Times doing the next lesson. Have one or two Quiet Times meditating on Hebrews 12:1-15 and review the meaning of the Greek word *paideuo*. Use Colossians 3:12-21 and 2 Timothy 2:22-26 also.

3. Plan a one-hour father-daughter or father-son time with one of your children or grandchildren. If you do not have children, choose a niece, nephew, or younger sibling. Building into the lives of children is the responsibility of every man. Be prepared to report back to the group.

4. These lessons have more reading. Use a highlighter or underline key parts to facilitate writing your own *Points to Remember.*

✓ End in group prayer using the *WAR* method. Spend some time praying for your children.

Leader's Guide to

LESSON 6 THE TONGUE HAS THE POWER OF LIFE AND DEATH

NOTE TO NEW LEADERS

You can download the Leader's Guide from the website *www.EveryManAWarrior.com* to make it easier to follow while leading the lesson.

THE TONGUE HAS THE POWER OF LIFE AND DEATH

✓ Break into pairs and recite all your verses to each other.

✓ Sign off on the *Completion Record.*

✓ Ask someone to open the session with prayer.

✓ Go around the room, asking each man to share one Quiet Time.

★✓ Go around the room, asking each man to share how his father-son or father-daughter time went. Ask: "What did you do? Where did you go?" Use the criteria listed on the right. Ask what he is learning about being a better father. Why?

✓ Begin reading the lesson paragraph by paragraph.

✓ Pages 83-91: Ask each of the questions on these pages. Depending on time, have two to four people give their answer. Try to include everyone.

★✓ Page 86: *Break lesson here.* Remember to review verses; share Quiet Times, and report on your father-son or father-daughter time at the beginning of the

SUCCESSFUL FATHER-CHILD TIME

Did you:

- *Make it safe*
- *Ask questions*
- *Keep the focus on them*
- *Listen*
- *Pray over them*
- *Speak a "building block of truth" into their lives*

second week. Place Proverbs 18:21 in the front pocket of your *EMAW Verse Pack* and memorize it this week.

✓ Pages 91-92: Have each person read their *Points to Remember* and then read the *Assignment for Next Week.*

✓ Page 92: Place Proverbs 18:21 and Ephesians 6:4 in the front window of your *EMAW Verse Pack* and memorize them this week.

✓ Page 92: Plan a one-hour outing with one of your children or grandchildren and be prepared to report back to the group.

✓ End in group prayer using the *WAR* method. Spend some time praying for your children.

The Tongue Has the Power of Life and Death

EVERY MAN A WARRIOR

Jeff's son Jimmy was six years old and finishing his second year of playing soccer. On Saturday a rainstorm messed up the schedule and some teams didn't show up. Jimmy's team and another team of eight-year-old boys had both arrived with no one to play. The two coaches decided to have a practice game. It sounded like a good idea at the time.

At age eight, the older boys were significantly bigger, stronger, and faster. They quickly overran the smaller six-year-olds. The older boys loved it. They could easily steal the ball, run or pass down field, and overwhelm the little six-year-old goalie named Jimmy, Jeff's son.

Jeff was standing on the sideline watching his little boy try to defend the goal from the onslaught of the older team. The eight-year-olds began to score over and over while most of the younger boys just stopped trying. They didn't even help Jimmy defend the goal.

The parents of the older kids were yelling and praising their sons. It was great to see them succeed. All the yelling seemed to center on Jimmy. The parents went wild each time one of their sons scored. Jimmy felt those cheers were for his failure. The coaches should have stopped the game, but didn't.

Jeff moved down to the end of the field and was speaking encouragement to Jimmy, yet watched with sorrow as his son got overwhelmed time and time again by the strength and experience of the older boys.

Eventually, the bigger boys did not even play their positions. They stood near the goal waiting for one of their team to steal the ball and pass it down field. The only obstacle was the goalie. Jeff could feel the helplessness of his son.

Jimmy fought with the strength of someone twice his age. But when the scores reached 15-0, he was overwhelmed with defeat, slumped to his knees on the grass, and started to cry. Jeff ran onto the field, knelt down to his son's level, and held him in his arms. Then Jeff cried too.

The crowd went silent, finally seeing the little boy's pain. The game ended.

Jeff stayed kneeling on the ground, arms around his son for a long time. In the midst of the tears Jeff kept saying these words, "Son, I'm so proud of you. That was totally unfair, and to see you fight so hard without any help makes me so proud of you."

Last year, Jimmy played football as a high school senior. He was chosen as homecoming king during the football game. He's a secure young man and liked by everyone. His success, at least in part, is because of the words spoken to him that day. *"The tongue has the power of life and death"* (Proverbs 18:21).

Jody came from an intellectual family. Her father had a Ph.D. and wanted his kids to succeed. Jody was easy to be around, competent, smart, and aggressive. I met her when I was in Romania. She traveled from the U.S. to minister to the women in Eastern Europe.

During that summer, our missionary team took a week in Stroudsburg, Austria, to pray, evaluate, and plan for the next year. I noticed that whenever Jody was asked to report on her responsibilities, her countenance would change. She seemed fearful, uneasy.

When I asked what was going on, she replied, "Oh, I hate evaluation and planning meetings. It reminds me too much of showing my report card to my dad. No matter if I had all A+s, which I mostly did, my dad would point out the one A- and say, 'Jody, if you had just worked a little harder, you could have done better and made an A+.' I felt like I could never measure up." I still remember the hurt in her eyes when she told me that story.

Today, Jody is married, has a family and a Ph.D. of her own. I doubt if her accomplishments have erased the pain she still feels from not being able to measure up in her dad's eyes. *"The tongue has the power of life and death"* (Proverbs 18:21).

Children will always try to rise to the level of expectation they believe you have for them.

The principles discussed in these lessons apply to grandfathers too. In fact, grandfathers can have almost as much impact on a child as the father. One grandfather quite proudly told me this story. On the Fourth of July he was watching his three grandchildren, two boys and a girl. One ten-year-old boy, like most ten-year-old boys, wasn't very wise. He lit a firecracker and tossed it at his twelve-year-old sister. Grandpa saw it and went into action. He jumped from his chair, grabbed the young man, and got in his face yelling, "If I ever see you do that again, I'll kick your butt so hard that. . .$#%^&!"

He felt he had handled the situation well, since this is the way he had been raised. I'm sure the grandson heard a message that day. *"There must be something terribly wrong with me for Grandpa to yell at me in this way."* I suspect the only thing he learned was to stay away from Grandpa. *"The tongue has the power of life and death"* (Proverbs 18:21).

Using Words to Build into a Child's Life

If the grandfather had understood the principle of Proverbs 18:21, he could have seen this as an opportunity to build into his grandson. He could have calmly called the boy over and talked to him about safety, or taught him something about consequences by having him sit out of the fun for a few minutes.

Or, he could have done what I've seen some really wise fathers do: speak a "positive building block of self-esteem" into their children or grandchildren's lives. He could have called the boy over and said, "Son, you're a better man than that. You could have badly injured your sister. I want you to go apologize to her." *"The tongue has the power of life and death"* (Proverbs 18:21).

Children will always try to rise to the level of expectation they believe you have for them. So watch out what thoughts you, or someone else, sow into your children's minds.

When my two girls were young, we often played in the yard together. Our next-door neighbor always had a zinger. "Oh you wait till your children are teenagers. Then you're going to have problems. You'll find out how awful teenagers can be." If a child hears a statement like that a few dozen times, especially from you, you can bet it will come true. You've already programmed them with the standard they will rise to.

One time after hearing this negative statement, I saw that my daughters had heard these words and were thinking about them. I called my girls over and said adamantly, "I don't believe that. You girls are fantastic, you are going to be incredible teenagers, and God is going to use you to do great things!" *"The tongue has the power of life and death"* (Proverbs 18:21).

Words That Hurt, Words That Build

In the last lesson we learned one of the most important truths about raising good kids. Your children get their self-image from what they believe Dad thinks about them. The most significant part of their beliefs about themselves comes from the words spoken out of your mouth! *"The tongue has the power of life and death"* (Proverbs 18:21).

✓ Review the stories above. What thoughts were being built into the self-image of each child? What impact do you think it had on the child?

Into Jimmy by his dad, Jeff:

Into Jody by her dad:

Into the grandson by his grandfather:

Into the two girls by the neighbor:

Into the two girls by their dad:

✓ Write down your own stories. Think back to your childhood and jot down one positive and one negative statement spoken to you. Write how it was said and what the circumstances were. Then jot down how those words impacted your life. Be ready to share.

Positive Story or Statement

Statement:

Circumstances:

How I was impacted by that statement:

Negative Story or Statement

Statement:

Circumstances:

How I was impacted by that statement:

The tongue has the power of life and death.

Proverbs 18:21

✓ Meditate on Proverbs 18:21. Study the examples below. Write two examples of how you could speak life into one of your children.

✓ Write two examples of speaking death (hurt) into a child.

Special note: This father had never trained his son in car maintenance. You cannot legitimately criticize your children for something you have never trained them in (see Ephesians 6:4).

Examples

Speaking life:

"Honey, you are growing into a beautiful young woman. Some man is going to be so lucky to marry you someday."

"Son, that was a great job you did changing the headlight of the car!"

Speaking death:

"I pity the man who ends up marrying you!"

"What, there's no water in your car radiator? Didn't you check it?

Do not let any unwholesome talk come out of your mouths, but only what is helpful for building others up according to their needs, that it may benefit those who listen.

—Ephesians 4:29

✓ Meditate on Ephesians 4:29. How does this verse relate to raising children?

★**Break here if you are spending two weeks on the lesson.**

The Anger of Man Does Not Work

"For the anger of man does not work [accomplish] the righteousness of God"

James 1:20 RSV.

Sally was away at college, partying and making some bad choices. Sally's dad, Denny, spent most of her childhood building his business, rarely spending any time with her. Her self-image was low as evidenced by the way she dressed, the guys she hung out with, and her *"I don't care"* attitude.

When she and her boyfriend moved in together, Denny came to see me. We began to meet each week and over the next six months, Denny worked at having weekly father-daughter time. At first she was skeptical, since over the years the only attention she had gotten from Dad was anger. (Once again, this had been how Denny was raised. His dad was an angry, harsh man, and Denny had learned to stay out of his way.)

Denny and Sally began making progress. He began to see the years he had wasted by not being involved in her life more deeply. When he realized that Sally was acting out the scars on her heart that he had put there by his absence and anger, it hit him like a ton of bricks.

But Denny was changing. He had learned to make their father-daughter time safe and a fun place for Sally to be. He had learned to ask questions and had proven to Sally that he would not blow up. They were having significant talks about life, sex, purpose, and God. Sally looked forward to their time together and Denny discovered something he had never known before. He could actually enjoy his children, and his time with Sally was sometimes the happiest time of his week.

A man's anger in raising children almost never brings about the change he wants, and many times it does just the opposite.

Sally's live-in boyfriend, Les, was a huge disappointment to Denny. He kept dropping out of school and getting fired from his food-service jobs because he often overslept and really didn't want to work. He sponged food, rent, and beer off Sally. Les had no car, so he constantly borrowed hers.

One night after some drinking, Les wrecked and totaled her car. This was the straw that broke the camel's back. Denny blew up at his daughter, shouting his disappointment in Sally and the choices she had made. The exchange left Sally in tears and Denny drove home in a rage. He called me to blow off some steam and confess how he had messed up. *"For the anger of man does not work [accomplish] the righteousness of God"* (James 1:20).

Over the next few days as Denny got the car towed out of the impound lot and dealt with the insurance company, his relationship with Sally got worse. She acted as if she couldn't care less about what had happened. She got a ride to school from a friend and did not return his calls. If anything, the incident had strengthened her relationship with Les.

In raising my own children and mentoring other men on the same issue, I've discovered an interesting result from a man's anger. *It almost never brings about the change he wants, and many times does just the opposite.*

James 1:20 describes how anger does *not* work in accomplishing the righteousness of God. The word *righteousness* means *"right, just, and wise."* In fact, it was formerly spelled *"rightwiseness,"* which clearly expresses its meaning.[1]

1 W. E. Vine, *Vine's Complete Expository Dictionary of Old and New Testament Words* (Nashville, TN: Thomas Nelson, 1996).

Denny wanted his daughter to change, to be more responsible, to grow up and make better decisions, to live with more *"right, wise" thinking.* But his anger brought about *the complete opposite effect.*

His anger took the focus off Sally and her decisions, and made the car wreck about Denny. Sally was so hurt by his anger that she wasn't even thinking about the car or her decisions. Her total focus was on one thing: *Dad is angry and doesn't care about me.* If Denny had not gotten mad, the problem of the wrecked car could have been left with Sally and Les. He could have calmly asked what they were going to do about their dilemma. It would have changed the whole outcome. It would have forced Sally and Les to deal with the consequences they were facing because of their decisions. In fact, it could have opened up some great father-daughter discussions about life, responsibility, relationships, and money.

As it was, it separated Denny and Sally and drove her into a deeper commitment to Les. The anger of a man almost never brings about the right-wise outcome that you and I desire, and many times does the exact opposite.

✓ Do you agree with the above statement on anger? Why or why not? Give an example of how you have observed this principle.

✓ How did anger play a role in the outcome of the previous story? Where did Denny's anger cause Sally to focus? How did it make her feel?

✓ Write the *Three Biblical Principles on Raising Children* from Lesson 5 on the next page. Jot down a thought about how each principle applies to Denny and his relationship with Sally.

Principle	*How It Applies*
1.	
2.	
3.	

Words That Build

I want to close this chapter by talking more about words that build. In Lesson 5 we looked at the *Three Biblical Principles of Raising Children.* All three come together under the concept of being able to speak *"words that build into a child."* My favorite passage on this subject is Proverbs 24:3-4. It is an analogy of how a house or family is built and how the children in that home can become *"rare and beautiful treasures."*

> ***By wisdom a house is built, and through understanding it is established; through knowledge its rooms are filled with rare and beautiful treasures.***
>
> ***—Proverbs 24:3-4***

✓ What role does wisdom, knowledge, and understanding have in creating children that are "rare and beautiful treasures"? Jot down your thoughts.

I often tell men when we are discussing a problem or situation they have with their children: "These are not problems. These are God-given opportunities to build into your child." Once you fully grasp the *Three Biblical Principles on Raising Children* you can see how a ten-year-old boy throwing a firecracker at his sister is really an opportunity to build wisdom or self-image into his life by saying: "Son, you are a better man than that."

Even a rebuke can build into your son or daughter if it is done wisely and without anger. Remember, your children deeply long for your approval and want to please you. When you tell your son that you know he is a better man than his actions show, on the inside he is secretly pleased that you believe in him. And in his God-given design he will want to rise to your expectation. Remember, the words spoken to a child will determine his destiny.

Over the years I've learned that every son yearns deeply to hear words from dad that communicate the following:

- ***Son, I love you and I'm proud of you.***
- ***Son, I believe you have what it takes to make it as a man.***
- ***Son, you have a good mind, the ability to think and be a success.***
- ***God's hand is on your life, and He is going to use you in a significant way.***

Every daughter yearns deeply to hear words similar to these from her father:

- ***Sweetie, you are special and beautiful. Some man will be so fortunate to marry you someday.***
- ***It is a joy to be around you and to spend time with you.***
- ***I love you, and I always want you to feel safe and protected.***
- ***God's hand is on your life and He is going to use you in a special way.***

✓ If sons and daughters hear these messages on a regular basis, what kind of person do you think they will become?

✓ Why do you say different things to your son and to your daughter?

✓ List the names of each of your children or grandchildren. Which of the above statements do they most need to hear from you? How will you begin to say these things to them?

✓ Review the lesson, organize your thoughts, and jot down the most important *Points to Remember* from this lesson. Be prepared to share what you wrote.

Points to Remember

1.

2.

3.

4.

Points that others shared that I want to remember:

Assignment for Next Week

1. Place Proverbs 18:21 and Ephesians 6:4 in the front pocket of your *EMAW Verse Pack* and memorize them this week.

2. Have your Quiet Times in the book of Proverbs, chapters 13, 17, 22, and 29:1-9. Record your thoughts and note any principles for raising children.

3. Have a one-hour time with one of your children. Communicate one of the messages from the list on page 90. Ask God to show you the impact of that statement. Review the *Principles for a Successful Father-Son or-Daughter Time* from lesson 5 and be ready to report back.

4. These lessons have more reading. Use a highlighter or underline key parts to facilitate writing your own *Points to Remember.*

✓ End in group prayer using the *WAR* method. Spend some time praying for your children.

Leader's Guide to

LESSON 7 THE TEENAGE YEARS: WHO'S IN CONTROL?

NOTE TO NEW LEADERS

You can download the Leader's Guide from the website *www.EveryManAWarrior.com* to make it easier to follow while leading the lesson.

THE TEENAGE YEARS: WHO'S IN CONTROL?

✓ Break into pairs and recite all your verses to each other.

✓ Sign off on the *Completion Record.*

✓ Ask someone to open the session with prayer.

✓ Go around the room, asking each man to share one Quiet Time.

★✓ Go around the room asking each man to share how his father-son or father-daughter time went. Ask: "What did you do? Where did you go? What did you talk about?" Use the criteria listed on the right. Ask what he is learning about being a better father. Why?

✓ Begin reading the lesson paragraph by paragraph.

✓ Pages 95-104: Ask each of the questions on these pages. Depending on time, have two to four people give their answer. Try to include everyone.

★✓ Page 100: *Break lesson here.* Remember to review verses, share Quiet Times, and report on your father-son or father-daughter time at the beginning of the second week.

SUCCESSFUL FATHER-CHILD TIME

Did you:

- *Make it safe*
- *Ask questions*
- *Keep the focus on them*
- *Listen*
- *Pray over them*
- *Speak a "building block of truth" into their lives*

✓ Pages 103-104: Have everyone read their *Points to Remember.* Discuss whenever possible. Read the *Assignment.*
✓ Page 104: Plan a one-hour outing with one of your children or grandchildren and be prepared to report back to the group.
✓ Page 104: Place the verse Proverbs 18:13 in the front pocket of your *EMAW Verse Pack* and memorize it this week.
✓ End in group prayer using the *WAR* method. Spend some time praying for your children.

Who's in Control?

EVERY MAN A WARRIOR

I first met Mark and Samantha in their church. Mark was a good leader, but he sometimes gravitated toward control as his leadership style. This was especially apparent when his daughter Lori turned fourteen. In junior high the school had started having dances and Mark made a rule, "No dating until you are sixteen, and that's final."

Lori's friends were having dates but at fourteen none of the kids could drive, so their moms or dads were always around or somehow involved in the event. In high school the pairing off by Lori's friends was even more intense. Lori was outgoing and liked by most everyone, but with each potential dating opportunity, Mark would overrule and quite forcefully reiterated his "no dating until you are sixteen" rule. Samantha saw Lori's humiliation at being the only girl among her peers who had never had a date. Unfortunately, neither Mark nor Samantha saw the deep resentment growing inside Lori.

Lori felt the rule was totally unfair. She was embarrassed when her friends asked her why she couldn't date. It seemed like Dad must not trust her. Each time she tried to discuss with him how she felt, the debate ended in angry words and tears. Mark felt that his leadership was being challenged; after all, he was just trying to protect his daughter. Communication between them stopped completely.

When the big sixteenth birthday came, Mark and Samantha gave Lori a party. There was a sigh of relief since the rule would no longer be in effect. Mark and Samantha hoped that things could go back to the way they were. No more fighting over dating. But little did they know of the problems that were coming.

Lori seemed somewhat happier. Her birthday party was a huge success. A number of young men came that Mark and Samantha had never met. They dressed and looked a little weird, making Lori's parents feel a bit uncomfortable—since the boys obviously had some interest in their daughter.

But the biggest unforeseen surprise came in the following weeks. Lori had a date almost every night. Now that she could drive, the dates took place after school or she and her date met at some other function. Many of the young men were unknown, new names to Mark and Samantha. Lori was almost never home. Her parents could not get a straight answer from her about who she was with or where. They suspected that many times she lied.

When the parents did meet some of her boyfriends, they were really concerned. Most did not seem to be the kind of guys they hoped she would gravitate toward. Now they had fights about curfews and where she went and with whom. She seemed to hate being home and to their dismay and grief, she sometimes stayed out all night.

I watched with deep sorrow the breakdown of communication between Lori and her parents. Unfortunately, Mark was imitating the 1950s style of parenting his father had used. He never looked for or saw other options. Samantha was the first to have suspicions. Lori felt sick and seemed more tired than normal. At 17, Lori was pregnant. When Mark got the news he wept.

✓ What thoughts do you have on the above story? List at least three observations.

✓ What do you think about Mark's idea that his dating rules would protect his daughter? How did it make Lori feel?

✓ Why do you think communication stopped between Lori and her parents?

✓ Lesson 5 introduced *Three Biblical Principles on Raising Children.* How could these parenting principles have helped Mark? How could he have applied them? Jot down your thoughts below on each.

- ***It is a father's God-given responsibility to train his children.***

—Ephesians 6:4

- ***Children get their self-image from what they believe Dad thinks about them.***

—Proverbs 17:6

- ***The words spoken to a child will determine his or her destiny.***

—Proverbs 18:21

The Result of Control

Why is control a bad parenting strategy for raising teenagers? Control has to be age-appropriate. When our children are first born, of course we need to control almost every element of their lives to protect them. However, if we want them to mature as teenagers, control can actually be a hindrance for their development into responsible adults.

When my daughters turned thirteen, I had this conversation with them during father-daughter time: "You know, young lady, becoming a teenager means you are moving quickly toward being an adult. So Mom and I are going to begin to make a few less decisions for you, and you will be making more of your own decisions." At thirteen, we gave them complete control over their annual clothing budget. Each year, we turned something else over to them. We provided a safe, loving environment for them to learn but let them make mistakes and live with the consequences.

We all learn much, much more from our mistakes than our successes. If we don't let our children think, make decisions, or fail they will never learn. We handicap our children in their abilities to reason, weigh different options, and make good decisions.

When a parent has a control strategy for his teenager, it usually has two extremely negative, unforeseen consequences:

- *First, it can overshadow or delete completely the number-one biblical responsibility of parents: the training of their children.*

- *Second, it means the parent is making the decisions instead of the child. It cheats the child out of lessons to be learned by the decision-making process.*

Focus on Training

Instead of focusing on controlling our teenagers, our focus should be on their training, their ability to think, and their capacity to make good decisions without our help. This way over time they gain experience in learning the consequences, both good and bad, of those decisions. This is also the road to becoming a self-sufficient, responsible adult.

When we as parents make control our objective, then every issue becomes about us. We're doing the choosing; we're making the decisions for the teenager. But, when we make their training the issue, every decision focuses on them and the possible consequences they will face. This process should start a few years before they become teenagers.

When my own children were in grade school, I often prayed that if they were making bad decisions they would get caught. I wanted them to learn consequences before the cost of those bad decisions was too high.

In control-oriented families the first really big decisions children start making on their own occur when they are teenagers. At this stage of life, those decisions are most likely made when the parents are not around and they often involve alcohol, sex, or drugs. If our children have not had experience making their own decisions and suffering the consequences, then the cost of bad choices with sex, drugs, and alcohol can be exceedingly high.

Instead of focusing on controlling our teenagers, our focus should be on their training, their ability to think, and their capacity to make good decisions without our help.

✓ What are your thoughts on the two unforeseen consequences from having a control strategy for parenting teenagers? Jot down at least one thought on each.

• *First, it can overshadow or delete completely the number one biblical responsibility of parents: the training of their children.*

• *Second, it means the parent is making the decisions instead of the child. It cheats the child out of lessons to be learned by the decision-making process.*

When my oldest daughter, Stephanie, turned thirteen, boys started hanging around our house. We took Stephanie and her male friends to the mall, to movies, or to the park. Most of the time we found reasons to stay close or made our basement the place for movies and pizza.

I made it a habit to get a father-daughter time within two to three days of each of these boy-girl outings. I wanted to talk about what she was learning about boys and relationships. Over time, the Lord taught me a very effective teaching method for teenagers: *ask questions, then shut up and listen.*

I remember when she was sixteen. We were at Burger King discussing her most recent and most serious relationship with some young man. The pattern for these talks on dating had been established, and now we had progressed into the real stuff. It was time to ask more serious questions.

I started the discussion with this statement: "Stephanie, you are becoming a beautiful young woman, and some man is going to be so lucky to marry you someday. What things do you like about Johnny?" There was a pause as she blushed and then said, "I don't know, he's cute." We both laughed, and after a few moments I asked a second question: "What kind of man do you want to marry someday?" There was another pause, but a more serious reply of, "I don't know."

This process of helping our children learn how to think is one of the greatest gifts we can give them.

Over the next few years, I asked many questions. Do you want to marry a man who is spiritual, or is that important to you? What stage of commitment are you at with this guy? Do you feel safe with this guy? What boundaries do you have on the physical aspect of your relationship? How does he treat his mom? How does his dad treat women? (Because if you marry this guy, that's how he will treat you.) Will he earn enough money for you to stay with the children, or do you want to work also after you have children?

These questions were asked over a two-to-three-year period of father-daughter times. The vast majority went unanswered when they were asked. But these became the questions my daughter thought about, wrestled with, and discussed with her circle of girlfriends.

Much of parenting during the teen years is about helping our children learn how to think for themselves. Good questions are an excellent vehicle to accomplish this.

Many times the questions came back to me after my daughters had contemplated them and gotten their friends' thoughts as well. This led to some substantial discussions. It was an opportunity to give examples from my own life on dating, marriage, boundaries, and values. The question sometimes was, "What did you and Mom do?" Within reason, I shared both mistakes and successes. I also shared stories from other couples, their decisions both good and bad, and then the consequences of those decisions. It was a time to let my children learn from our regrets, and perhaps avoid repeating some of them.

I've had dozens of discussions like this with my daughters. We've talked about men, money, relationships, cars, other people's opinions of us, self-worth, their walk with God, wounded people, and handling life's disappointments. We've also just laughed and had fun.

My objective was not to tell them what to do or think. My objective was to plant a seed and develop their ability to think about these questions of life. *This process of helping our children learn how to think is one of the great-*

est gifts we can give them. But it only happens if we have safe and open communications with them.

Having a strategy of control kills communication and teaches our teenagers to hide things from us. Once that happens, our ability to influence them almost dies completely.

★ **Break here if you are spending two weeks on the lesson.**

What's Really Going On? Find Out by Asking Questions

Asking questions is an important skill to use in discovering what's really going on inside your child. Proverbs 18:13 is one of my key verses on good parenting: *"He who answers before listening—<u>that is his folly and his shame</u>"* (emphasis added). Speaking too quickly, without really knowing what is going on inside your child, is a big mistake. We end up fighting the wrong issues.

My friend Jake is a good example. Jake and his wife, Candice, have two great kids. Everything was going well until their daughter, Michaela, reached junior high. She began to break all the rules, misbehave, and disobey. She was driving her parents crazy. Jake had to work long hours as an investment banker. After work, he spent time every night coaching his son's baseball team, competing for the regional championship. His son, David, was the pitcher, and when they didn't have a game he practiced with Dad or they went to the batting cages.

Sometimes when Jake arrived home, Candice was in tears from fighting with Michaela. Jake would get angry and have to discipline her. The parents were at their wits' end, so Jake came to see me and related what was happening. As I asked questions, Jake told me one thing that turned on the light. During one conversation when Mom asked, "What's wrong?" Michaela had blurted out these words: "Dad's always mad at me and he spends all his time with David!"

That weekend Jake took Michaela out for dinner and a movie, just the two of them. Afterward, Michaela was almost a perfect angel for the next few weeks.

Speaking too quickly, without really knowing what is going on inside your child, is a big mistake. We end up fighting the wrong issues.

What was really going on? Michaela was feeling left out, that David was more important to Dad, and the only way she got any attention was by misbehaving. This was the real issue. Mom had stumbled onto it by asking questions.

Remember, children get their self-image from what they believe Dad thinks about them. When Dad is absent or uncommunicative, the message is clear: *"I'm not valued, loved, or important to him."* This message is absorbed and becomes what the daughter believes about herself: *I am not valuable, worthy of love, wanted, or special. I do not deserve to be cherished.* When these messages are sent over a long period of time, our teenage daughter will find a place where she does feel loved, wanted, and valued. Unfortunately, that is usually in the arms of a man who takes advantage of the situation.

Asking questions communicates value to your teenager. It says, "I value you, your mind, your ability to think, your opinion." When I don't ask, but just tell or command, control becomes the issue, and once again, we and the child both lose. It forces the teenager into fighting for independence and rebelling against this atmosphere of control.

Make it your objective to always ask at least one question of your child before making a decision. Sometimes the best question is, "What do you think?"

You and I want our teenagers to become independent, responsible adults. But this independence needs to be based on the wisdom and maturity that comes from making decisions and living with the consequences, not from a desire to escape from the smothering control of parents. Changing the way we parent is not an easy task. It takes time, energy, and prayer! Once again, much of our default mode is how we ourselves were parented.

He who answers before listening—that is his folly and his shame.

—Proverbs 18:13

✓ Meditate on Proverbs 18:13 using the *Ask Questions* method. Jot down your thoughts. What does it say about a parent who does most of the talking?

Ask Questions

Is there:

A command to obey

A promise to claim

A sin to avoid

An application to make

Something new about God

Ask: Who, What, When, Where, Why

Emphasize:
Different words

Rewrite:
In your own words

✓ The verse above uses two strong words—folly and shame—about drawing conclusions without asking questions. What do these words mean to you?

✓ In parenting, what do you think is the purpose of listening?

✓ Rewrite Proverbs 18:13 in your own words.

Parents who make control their objective unknowingly communicate the following messages to their children:

- ***You don't know how to think; therefore I must do the thinking for you.***
- ***I don't want you to suffer the consequences for your bad decisions. Therefore when I'm in control, I will bail you out of your problems.***
- ***I don't believe you have what it takes to make good decisions or be successful.***
- ***I don't trust you. You are not responsible. Therefore I need to control you.***

Trying to control our teenagers imprisons them in permanent adolescence, destroys their self-esteem, fosters resentment, and stifles maturity.[1]

1 Adapted from Foster Cline and Jim Fay, Parenting with Love and Logic (Colorado Springs, CO: NavPress, 2006).

Parents who make training their children the objective want to:

- ***Help their children learn how to think and make decisions.***
- ***Help their children learn the consequences of those decisions.***
- ***Cause their children to believe they can succeed.***
- ***Give their children the freedom to mature.***
- ***Keep communication lines open and the focus on the relationship.***

✓ Review the lists above about control versus training. Write a paragraph comparing a control strategy versus a training strategy for raising teenagers.

✓ Review the lesson, organize your thoughts, and jot down the most important points to remember from this lesson. Be prepared to share what you wrote.

Points to Remember

1.

2.

3.

4.

Points that others shared that I want to remember:

Assignment for Next Week

1. ✓ Place Proverbs 18:13 in the front pocket of your *EMAW Verse Pack* and memorize it this week.

2. Have your Quiet Times on the following passages: Ecclesiastes 11:9–12:14; Proverbs 23:1-28; Proverbs 24:1-34.

3. Plan a one-hour father-daughter or father-son time with one of your children or grandchildren. Be prepared to report back to the group.

4. These lessons have more reading. Use a highlighter or underline key parts to facilitate writing your own *Points to Remember.*

5. It is time to reflect and review. Do the *Proficiency Evaluation* for lessons 1–8. Try to fill in the answers without looking first. Then go back to find and check your answers. Finish any lessons that you have not completed.

✓ End in group prayer using the *WAR* method. Spend some time praying for your children.

Leader's Guide to

LESSON 8

Turning the Hearts of Children to Their Fathers

Note to New Leaders

You can download the Leader's Guide from the website *www.EveryManAWarrior.com* to make it easier to follow while leading the lesson.

Turning the Hearts of Children to Their Fathers

★✓ Break into pairs and recite all your verses to each other. Count the number of recorded Quiet Times you have in the back of the book. You should have twenty or more. Sign off on the *Completion Record.*

✓ Ask someone to open the session with prayer.

✓ Go around the room asking each man to share one Quiet Time.

★✓ Go around the room asking each man to share how his father-son or father-daughter time went. Ask: "What did you do? Where did you go? What did you talk about?" Use the criteria listed on the right. Ask what he is learning about being a better father. Why?

✓ Begin reading the lesson paragraph by paragraph.

✓ Pages 109-116: Ask each of the questions on these pages. Depending on time, have two to four people give their answer. Try to include everyone.

Successful Father-Child Time

Did you:

- *Make it safe*
- *Ask questions*
- *Keep the focus on them*
- *Listen*
- *Pray over them*
- *Speak a "building block of truth" into their lives*

★✓ Page 111: *Break lesson here.* Remember to review verses, share Quiet Times, and report on your father-son or father-daughter time at the beginning of the second week.

✓ Pages 113-115: Answer each of the *Proficiency Evaluation* questions. Discuss whenever possible.

✓ Pages 116-117: Have everyone read their *Points to Remember.* Read the *Assignment* together.

✓ Page 117: Place the verse 1 Peter 3:8-9 in the front pocket of your *EMAW Verse Pack* and memorize it this week. Plan a one-hour outing with one of your children or grandchildren and be prepared to report back to the group.

✓ End in group prayer using the *WAR* method. Spend some time praying for your children and for healing that needs to happen in your relationship with them.

Turning the Hearts of Children to Their Fathers

Paul was fifty-one years old and his third marriage was on the rocks. He knew his pattern of drinking and long hours at the office was once again shattering his dreams of sharing his life with someone special.

Paul admitted that his first two marriages had ended because of his own stupidity. Drinking, drugs, and other women had caused both wives to leave. The four children that were his never called and hardly spoke to him.

Driving home late one night, Paul decided to skip the bar and in his heart he said a silent prayer: *"Lord, can You help me?"* Unknown to Paul, his wife, Kate, had also begun to pray. Kate had grown up in a Christian home, but with the hurts of her own divorce and the disappointments of her life, she had not prayed in some time. Kate too knew that her marriage to Paul was faltering.

That night, through the unseen hand of God, Paul and Kate made a decision that they needed help and decided to go to church. Paul remembered attending an Alcoholics Anonymous meeting at a local church. He thought he could find it again, and that Sunday morning they nervously went to church together.

To their surprise, someone greeted them at the door and welcomed them. There were no pews, only well-padded chairs. The singing was upbeat and people smiled like they actually wanted to be there. For Paul, this was totally unexpected.

During the next few weeks Paul and Kate made church a weekly event and looked forward to going. One Sunday, the speaker made an announcement about a busload of guys all going to a stadium for a men-only conference on "Being a Better Man." Paul was intrigued. He knew he needed to change and being a better man seemed like the right direction. He signed up.

The first night of the conference, a man carried a huge log to the podium. As he told the story of his own broken life, he slowly, methodically built a cross. As he swung his ax he shared how the death of a man named Jesus, on such a cross, had changed his life. The speaker explained that the death of Jesus had paid for all of the man's mistakes and that by giving his life to Jesus he had been able to nail his sins, his problems, and his hurts to that cross.

Paul was overwhelmed; the man was speaking to him! At an invitation for men to come down and nail their own mistakes to the cross, Paul left his seat and ran to the stage, his heart bursting inside. He knew he had made a mess of his life and family, and he desperately wanted to change. That night as Paul knelt before the cross, God changed him for all eternity.

Through a friend, Paul was asked to join a discipleship Bible study. The study required that he have a daily Quiet Time and memorize a verse of the Bible each week. Paul loved it. Over time, memorizing and meditating on the Scripture, Paul began a transformation process that gave him a whole new life.

In the next five years, Paul memorized and studied the Scripture and began to meet and disciple other men. Kate joined a women's Bible study and was growing. Together Paul and Kate began to live their lives for one thing—loving Jesus and passing that love on to the people around them.

During this time of growing spiritually, Paul began to pray for his children. He begged God to forgive him of the pain he had caused and the wounds he had left on their hearts. Paul began to ask the Lord for a way to win them back.

The following Christmas, Paul sent each of his children a gift and wrote them a letter telling them what God had done in his life. At the end of each letter he asked for forgiveness and told them he loved them. Paul and Kate prayed that God would speak to the hearts of his children.

God was at work, and on Christmas day Karen, one of his children, called and thanked Paul for the gift. Since they had not talked for some time, Paul asked about her life. This was a shock to Karen, since her dad had never asked before. The call was uncomfortable, but they talked for seven minutes. It was a start.

Paul was very wise during the years of this rebuilding process. He never preached, but he loved and accepted his children for who they were.

About a week later, Paul called Karen and asked her to lunch. Karen was hesitant. She thought she could bear the presence of this man for a short lunch since he had promised to let her choose the restaurant. As a college student, she could not afford to eat out much. Karen agreed to meet at Sortino's Pizza, her favorite place just off campus. If Dad was still a jerk, at least she would get a good meal.

During one of Paul's Quiet Times, the Lord had spoken to him from Proverbs 28:13: *"He who conceals his sins does not prosper, but whoever confesses and renounces them finds mercy."* Paul knew he needed to tell Karen how sorry he was for the way he had left her, her brother, and their mom. He asked the Lord to give him the right timing for such a conversation.

Karen was tense when they met. Facing each other in a booth, Karen could see that Paul was different. She had hardly ever seen him smile before, and the hardness around his eyes was gone. Paul opened the conversation with a question, "Karen, would you tell me about you?" To her surprise, he eagerly listened as she talked. He even asked if there was any way he could help. She quickly said no, because she was still unsure of who this man really was to her.

Their time ended after an hour. Paul said, "Thank you for seeing me. I so enjoyed our time." He waved as she got in her car, and as soon as she left, Paul thanked the Lord that the time had gone well.

Paul waited another month before he asked Karen to lunch again. Another successful meeting—and Karen was not quite as tense being around her dad. These lunches became a regular event. Every two to three weeks Paul would call and ask her to lunch. Since Paul kept the conversation mostly about her, he was discovering the daughter he had never really known. Karen felt the huge ache in her heart slowly melting away, and she actually looked forward to their time.

He who conceals his sins does not prosper, but whoever confesses and renounces them finds mercy.

—Proverbs 28:13

During their fourth meeting, Karen blurted out a question, her voiced laced with hurt: "Why do you keep calling me? You never seemed to care before!" It was the opening that Paul had prayed for. There was a moment of silence with Paul looking into his daughter's hurting eyes. He cleared his throat, shot up a silent prayer, and responded: "Karen, I've been an awful dad over the years and I treated you, your brother, and your mom horribly. None of the things I did were ever your fault. Now that God is in my life, He is making me into a new man. I'm so very sorry that I hurt you and I would very much like to become the dad that you deserve and that I should have always been." Karen's eyes filled with tears. She hung her head and cried. "Okay, Dad," she said. It was the first time she had called him Dad. Then Paul cried too.

That conversation happened a number of years ago. Since then Paul and Karen have met almost every week. Karen began to tell her siblings about the changes in Dad. Their God-given desire to know their father eventually overcame their reluctance. One by one the other three accepted lunch invitations from Paul and started the rebuilding of a relationship.

Paul was very wise during the years of this rebuilding process. He never preached but simply loved and accepted them. Without Christ, each was coping with the pain in their lives by using alcohol or sex, the same coping patterns they had seen their dad use when they were small. Paul and Kate continued to pray.

The following Christmas all four children came together for a family meal. At the blessing Paul and Kate both reached out their hands. For the first time ever, the family held hands and Paul prayed a short prayer for each of them. Over time this became a family ritual. Now, years later, Paul opens each father-daughter or father-son meal with prayer, thanking God for the food but praying specifically for them. Karen always reaches out for her dad's hand when he prays.

✓ Review the story. Why do you think Paul was successful at winning back his children? Jot down at least three thoughts.

✓ How important do you think it was that Paul made apologies to his children? Why?

Over the years I have seen men *"win back their children."* I've seen others who have not. The ones who haven't succeeded generally are still trying to use a control pattern or they have not resolved the issues that drove their children away.

Paul was successful for a couple of reasons. He did not preach his newfound Christianity, but he loved and accepted his children for who they were. Jesus used this same strategy. People never felt condemned when they were around Him.

When you have wounded one of your children, you need to go and apologize! It takes a real man to say "I'm sorry" when he's blown it. This is not sign of weakness. It is an attribute of strength and maturity.

Paul also openly confessed his mistakes and never brought up theirs. Paul knew that his kids were acting out the scars he had put there. He also knew that their biggest need was to discover the love of Christ. He did not let some smaller issue become a stumbling block that would make him unsafe to be around or make them doubt that Christ really was the answer.

Some of you may have children who are not as close as you would want. Like Paul, you may long for that to change. Proverbs 18:19 is a favorite verse of mine on the impact of conflict. I've written it here in my own words. *"An offended brother [child, wife, or friend] is harder to win back than a city with walls"* (Proverbs 18:19).

A city with walls! What a good word picture for what happens between you and your child when a dispute gets out of hand.

True training and development in our children can only happen in the context of a relationship. When that relationship gets bruised, training stops and we both lose. A festering hurt between a parent and child puts a wall around the child's heart and the deeper the wound, the thicker the wall. This wall then causes the child to turn a deaf ear. They no longer hear what we have to say.

One of my children had the innate ability to push my buttons. Sometimes during those teenage years I responded in a way that was not my finest hour! You don't burn the house down to get rid of rats. Sometimes we as men have the ability to blow up and torch a relationship based on our own irritations. Remember James 1:20, "The anger of man does not work" (see Lesson 6).

When you have wounded one of your children, you need to go and apologize! It takes a real man to say "I'm sorry" when he's blown it. This is not sign of weakness. It is an attribute of strength and maturity.

I've seen a few men who have taken this attitude: *"That kid is the problem! He's at fault, so he should apologize to me first."* This is a symptom of some severe woundedness or immaturity. You're the man, you're the leader, and you are the model your kids will imitate. If you cannot say you're sorry to your children, they will be the same way. They too will have deeply wounded relationships that do not heal.

To my surprise, my apology always led to a strengthening of my relationship with my daughter. *When we make legitimate apologies to our children, it communicates that we highly value them.* Many times after my apology, my daughter would give me some additional information about what was going on in her life. Many times, the acting out was caused by some hurt she was feeling such as a rejection at school, problems with a friend or teacher, or something else hidden inside. Just like adults, kids take their hurt and frustrations out on those closest to them.

How you handle conflict with your child will become his or her grid for what is normal and right in handling conflict. If you handle conflict according to biblical principles, you will greatly enhance their future relationships.

✓ What do you see as some of the most important aspects of how to rebuild a broken relationship between a father and one of his children? Why?

✓ What impact does it have on the child if a father cannot apologize for his mistakes?

★ **Break here if you are spending two weeks on the lesson.**

Finally, all of you, live in harmony with one another; be sympathetic, love as brothers, be compassionate and humble. Do not repay evil with evil or insult with insult, but with blessing, because to this you were called so that you may inherit a blessing.

—1 Peter 3:8-9

Ask Questions

Is there:

A command to obey

A promise to claim

A sin to avoid

An application to make

Something new about God

Ask: Who, What, When, Where, Why

Emphasize:
Different words

Rewrite:
In your own words

✓ Meditate on 1 Peter 3:8-9 using the *Ask Questions* method. Jot down your observations below.

✓ Rewrite 1 Peter 3:8-9 in your own words.

Conclusions

We have just spent the last few weeks studying how to be a better father. There is much we did not cover. But if you apply the principles you have learned in these chapters, then *you too will develop into a better man* during these years of raising your children.

At the end of the Revolutionary War-era movie *The Patriot*, Benjamin Martin, played by Mel Gibson, confronts his British archrival Col. William Tavington, who had already killed two of Martin's sons. Martin fights Tavington in a vicious duel. Tavington manages to bring Ben to his knees, taunting, "It seems you are not the better man." Suddenly the tables turn. Just before Benjamin Martin rams the bayonet through his enemy's gullet he replies, *"My sons are better men!"*

Don't make it your goal that your kids have more possessions or have it easier than you did. Make it your goal that your children excel in character, are more secure in who they are, are equipped to walk with God, and better prepared for life than you were. Ask God for the grace to train them well so you, too, can say, *"My sons are better men."*

✓ Do the *Proficiency Evaluation* and write your *Points to Remember* to complete the lesson.

Proficiency Evaluation
Marriage and Raising Children
Lessons 1–4: Marriage

✓ In Lesson 1, what was meant when the author describes some marriages as *"two ticks and no dog?"*

✓ Why is it *"not good"* for a man to be alone?

✓ The man carries a greater responsibility in the marriage. Is this statement true? Why or why not?

✓ *When a man sees his wife's perspective as wrong or invalid because it is different from his own and refuses to consider its merit, he's an*
______________________!

✓ Jot down the references to the three verses you have memorized on the topic of marriage.

✓ From Lesson 2, where do most men learn their leadership style in marriage?

✓ When a man is selfish in marriage and does not treat his wife as the Bible commands, then by his modeling he unknowingly teaches his sons to be ____

and his daughters to be ______________________________
because the message they saw modeled is: *"Men are selfish, so watch out for yourself."*

✓ The first step for a man to be a godly husband according to Ephesians 5:25, is ______________________________.

✓ For a woman the relationship she has with her dad, the first man in her life, creates a homing device that ______________________________ ______________________________ and how she interprets ______________________________ ______________________________ .

✓ God has given every man a special gift in marriage. Inside every woman is a God-given desire to ______________________________.

✓ Write out *My Marriage Commitment.*

LESSONS 5–8: RAISING CHILDREN

✓ Jot down the *Three Biblical Principles on Raising Children.*

1.

2.

3.

✓ The central theme of what the Bible teaches on raising children is ______________________________.

✓ What message is sent to a child when he or she is ignored? When you ask questions?

✓ What principles for a successful father-daughter or father-son time were learned in Lesson 5? List as many as you can.

1. 2.

3. 4.

5. 6.

✓ The tongue has the power of ______________________________.

✓ The anger of man almost never ______________________________ and many times does just the ______________________________.

✓ When the parent of a teenager has a control strategy, it has two negative consequences. List them.

1.

2.

✓ The process of helping our children learn how to ______________________________ is one of the greatest gifts we can give them.

✓ He who answers before listening, that is his ______________________________ and ______________________________.

✓ Review the lesson, organize your thoughts, and jot down the most important points to remember from this lesson. Be prepared to share what you wrote.

Points to Remember

1.

2.

3.

4.

Points that others shared that I want to remember:

Assignment for Next Week

1. ✓ Place 1 Peter 3:8-9 in the front window of your *EMAW Verse Pack* and memorize it this week.

2. Plan a one-hour father-daughter or father-son time with one of your children or grandchildren. Be prepared to report back to the group.

3. Have your Quiet Times in the following passages: 1 Thessalonians 2:6-13, 2 Timothy 2:1-13, 1 Corinthians 9:19-27, and Matthew 28:1-20.

4. These lessons have more reading. Use a highlighter or underline key parts to facilitate writing your own *Points to Remember.*

✓ End in group prayer using the *WAR* method. Spend some time praying for your children.

APPENDIX

THE EVERY MAN A WARRIOR ICON

The EVERY MAN A WARRIOR icon is a symbol of a man's Quiet Time. God intended for you to be a warrior that worships the person of Jesus Christ. Your Quiet Time is a place of worship; but also a place to get ready for battle. Make it your objective to spend enough time with Jesus each day to do both; worship and prepare for war. Each is an important part of who you are as a man.

I Am a Warrior and I Kneel at the Cross

I kneel at the cross, battered and bruised, with blood on my sword and a shield that is used. My helmet is off, my face is scarred. I'm weary and tired. I'm a warrior and I kneel at the cross.

I am also a prince and a son of the King, with power and authority to rule. But instead, I give up my life to serve because I'm a warrior and I kneel at the cross.

I live as a light in a dark world of pain. I fight to set captives free from their prison and shame. I battle for truth and I count the cost. I'm a warrior and I kneel at the cross.

I reject the world with its brokenness and loss, because He died for me upon that cross. Now I have HOPE and a lasting reward. I'm a warrior and I kneel at the cross.

I'm coming home soon when my battles are won. To see my father's face and hear, "Well done my son. You are home at last, take your place at my side; because I chose you to be a warrior and you knelt at the cross."

Lonnie Berger

Date ________________ Passage I Read Today ________________

Ask Questions

Is there:

A command to obey

A promise to claim

A sin to avoid

An application to make

Something new about God

Ask: Who, What, When, Where, Why

Emphasize:
Different words

Rewrite:
In your own words

Major themes from all I read.

Best verse and thought for the day. (Write the verse & your thoughts.)

Communicate With God

W - *Worship Him*

A - *Admit Sin*

R - *My Requests*

Date ________________ Passage I Read Today ________________

Ask Questions

Is there:

A command to obey

A promise to claim

A sin to avoid

An application to make

Something new about God

Ask: Who, What, When, Where, Why

Emphasize:
Different words

Rewrite:
In your own words

Major themes from all I read.

Best verse and thought for the day. (Write the verse & your thoughts.)

Communicate With God

W - *Worship Him*

A - *Admit Sin*

R - *My Requests*

Date ____________ Passage I Read Today ____________

Ask Questions

Is there:

A command to obey

A promise to claim

A sin to avoid

An application to make

Something new about God

Ask: Who, What, When, Where, Why

Emphasize:
Different words

Rewrite:
In your own words

Major themes from all I read.

Best verse and thought for the day. (Write the verse & your thoughts.)

Communicate With God

W - *Worship Him*

A - *Admit Sin*

R - *My Requests*

Date ____________ Passage I Read Today ____________

Ask Questions

Is there:

A command to obey

A promise to claim

A sin to avoid

An application to make

Something new about God

Ask: Who, What, When, Where, Why

Emphasize:
Different words

Rewrite:
In your own words

Major themes from all I read.

Best verse and thought for the day. (Write the verse & your thoughts.)

Communicate With God

W - *Worship Him*

A - *Admit Sin*

R - *My Requests*

Date ________________ Passage I Read Today ________________

Major themes from all I read.

Ask Questions

Is there:

A command to obey

A promise to claim

A sin to avoid

An application to make

Something new about God

Ask: Who, What, When, Where, Why

Emphasize:
Different words

Rewrite:
In your own words

Best verse and thought for the day. (Write the verse & your thoughts.)

Communicate *With God*

W - *Worship Him*

A - *Admit Sin*

R - *My Requests*

Date ________________ Passage I Read Today ________________

Major themes from all I read.

Ask Questions

Is there:

A command to obey

A promise to claim

A sin to avoid

An application to make

Something new about God

Ask: Who, What, When, Where, Why

Emphasize:
Different words

Rewrite:
In your own words

Best verse and thought for the day. (Write the verse & your thoughts.)

Communicate *With God*

W - *Worship Him*

A - *Admit Sin*

R - *My Requests*

Date ______________ Passage I Read Today ______________

Ask Questions

Is there:

A command to obey

A promise to claim

A sin to avoid

An application to make

Something new about God

Ask: Who, What, When, Where, Why

Emphasize:
Different words

Rewrite:
In your own words

Major themes from all I read.

Best verse and thought for the day. (Write the verse & your thoughts.)

Communicate With God

W - *Worship Him*

A - *Admit Sin*

R - *My Requests*

Date ______________ Passage I Read Today ______________

Ask Questions

Is there:

A command to obey

A promise to claim

A sin to avoid

An application to make

Something new about God

Ask: Who, What, When, Where, Why

Emphasize:
Different words

Rewrite:
In your own words

Major themes from all I read.

Best verse and thought for the day. (Write the verse & your thoughts.)

Communicate With God

W - *Worship Him*

A - *Admit Sin*

R - *My Requests*

Date ____________ Passage I Read Today ____________

Major themes from all I read.

Ask Questions

Is there:

A command to obey

A promise to claim

A sin to avoid

An application to make

Something new about God

Ask: Who, What, When, Where, Why

Emphasize: Different words

Rewrite: In your own words

Best verse and thought for the day. (Write the verse & your thoughts.)

Communicate With God

W - *Worship Him*

A - *Admit Sin*

R - *My Requests*

Date ____________ Passage I Read Today ____________

Major themes from all I read.

Ask Questions

Is there:

A command to obey

A promise to claim

A sin to avoid

An application to make

Something new about God

Ask: Who, What, When, Where, Why

Emphasize: Different words

Rewrite: In your own words

Best verse and thought for the day. (Write the verse & your thoughts.)

Communicate With God

W - *Worship Him*

A - *Admit Sin*

R - *My Requests*

Date ______________ Passage I Read Today ______________

Ask Questions

Is there:

A command to obey

A promise to claim

A sin to avoid

An application to make

Something new about God

Ask: Who, What, When, Where, Why

Emphasize:
Different words

Rewrite:
In your own words

Major themes from all I read.

Best verse and thought for the day. (Write the verse & your thoughts.)

Communicate With God

W - *Worship Him*

A - *Admit Sin*

R - *My Requests*

Date ______________ Passage I Read Today ______________

Ask Questions

Is there:

A command to obey

A promise to claim

A sin to avoid

An application to make

Something new about God

Ask: Who, What, When, Where, Why

Emphasize:
Different words

Rewrite:
In your own words

Major themes from all I read.

Best verse and thought for the day. (Write the verse & your thoughts.)

Communicate With God

W - *Worship Him*

A - *Admit Sin*

R - *My Requests*

Date ______________ Passage I Read Today ______________

Major themes from all I read.

Ask Questions

Is there:

A command to obey

A promise to claim

A sin to avoid

An application to make

Something new about God

Ask: Who, What, When, Where, Why

Emphasize:
Different words

Rewrite:
In your own words

Best verse and thought for the day. (Write the verse & your thoughts.)

Communicate *With God*

W - *Worship Him*

A - *Admit Sin*

R - *My Requests*

Date ______________ Passage I Read Today ______________

Major themes from all I read.

Ask Questions

Is there:

A command to obey

A promise to claim

A sin to avoid

An application to make

Something new about God

Ask: Who, What, When, Where, Why

Emphasize:
Different words

Rewrite:
In your own words

Best verse and thought for the day. (Write the verse & your thoughts.)

Communicate *With God*

W - *Worship Him*

A - *Admit Sin*

R - *My Requests*

Date ______________ Passage I Read Today ______________

Ask Questions

Is there:

A command to obey

A promise to claim

A sin to avoid

An application to make

Something new about God

Ask: Who, What, When, Where, Why

Emphasize:
Different words

Rewrite:
In your own words

Major themes from all I read.

Best verse and thought for the day. (Write the verse & your thoughts.)

Communicate *With God*

W - *Worship Him*

A - *Admit Sin*

R - *My Requests*

Date ______________ Passage I Read Today ______________

Ask Questions

Is there:

A command to obey

A promise to claim

A sin to avoid

An application to make

Something new about God

Ask: Who, What, When, Where, Why

Emphasize:
Different words

Rewrite:
In your own words

Major themes from all I read.

Best verse and thought for the day. (Write the verse & your thoughts.)

Communicate *With God*

W - *Worship Him*

A - *Admit Sin*

R - *My Requests*

Date ______________ Passage I Read Today ______________

Major themes from all I read.

Ask Questions

Is there:

A command to obey

A promise to claim

A sin to avoid

An application to make

Something new about God

Ask: Who, What, When, Where, Why

Emphasize:
Different words

Rewrite:
In your own words

Best verse and thought for the day. (Write the verse & your thoughts.)

Communicate With God

W - *Worship Him*

A - *Admit Sin*

R - *My Requests*

Date ______________ Passage I Read Today ______________

Major themes from all I read.

Ask Questions

Is there:

A command to obey

A promise to claim

A sin to avoid

An application to make

Something new about God

Ask: Who, What, When, Where, Why

Emphasize:
Different words

Rewrite:
In your own words

Best verse and thought for the day. (Write the verse & your thoughts.)

Communicate With God

W - *Worship Him*

A - *Admit Sin*

R - *My Requests*

Date ________________ Passage I Read Today ________________

Ask Questions

Is there:

A command to obey

A promise to claim

A sin to avoid

An application to make

Something new about God

Ask: Who, What, When, Where, Why

Emphasize:
Different words

Rewrite:
In your own words

Major themes from all I read.

Best verse and thought for the day. (Write the verse & your thoughts.)

Communicate *With God*

W - *Worship Him*

A - *Admit Sin*

R - *My Requests*

Date ________________ Passage I Read Today ________________

Ask Questions

Is there:

A command to obey

A promise to claim

A sin to avoid

An application to make

Something new about God

Ask: Who, What, When, Where, Why

Emphasize:
Different words

Rewrite:
In your own words

Major themes from all I read.

Best verse and thought for the day. (Write the verse & your thoughts.)

Communicate *With God*

W - *Worship Him*

A - *Admit Sin*

R - *My Requests*

Date____________ Passage I Read Today____________

Ask Questions

Is there:

A command to obey

A promise to claim

A sin to avoid

An application to make

Something new about God

Ask: Who, What, When, Where, Why

Emphasize:
Different words

Rewrite:
In your own words

Major themes from all I read.

Best verse and thought for the day. (Write the verse & your thoughts.)

Communicate With God

W - *Worship Him*

A - *Admit Sin*

R - *My Requests*

Date____________ Passage I Read Today____________

Ask Questions

Is there:

A command to obey

A promise to claim

A sin to avoid

An application to make

Something new about God

Ask: Who, What, When, Where, Why

Emphasize:
Different words

Rewrite:
In your own words

Major themes from all I read.

Best verse and thought for the day. (Write the verse & your thoughts.)

Communicate With God

W - *Worship Him*

A - *Admit Sin*

R - *My Requests*

Date ________________ Passage I Read Today ____________________

Ask Questions

Is there:

A command to obey

A promise to claim

A sin to avoid

An application to make

Something new about God

Ask: Who, What, When, Where, Why

Emphasize:
Different words

Rewrite:
In your own words

Major themes from all I read.

Best verse and thought for the day. (Write the verse & your thoughts.)

Communicate *With God*

W - *Worship Him*

A - *Admit Sin*

R - *My Requests*

Date ________________ Passage I Read Today ____________________

Ask Questions

Is there:

A command to obey

A promise to claim

A sin to avoid

An application to make

Something new about God

Ask: Who, What, When, Where, Why

Emphasize:
Different words

Rewrite:
In your own words

Major themes from all I read.

Best verse and thought for the day. (Write the verse & your thoughts.)

Communicate *With God*

W - *Worship Him*

A - *Admit Sin*

R - *My Requests*

Date ______________ Passage I Read Today ______________

Major themes from all I read.

Ask Questions

Is there:

A command to obey

A promise to claim

A sin to avoid

An application to make

Something new about God

Ask: Who, What, When, Where, Why

Emphasize:
Different words

Rewrite:
In your own words

Best verse and thought for the day. (Write the verse & your thoughts.)

C*ommunicate With God*

W - *Worship Him*

A - *Admit Sin*

R - *My Requests*

Date ______________ Passage I Read Today ______________

Major themes from all I read.

Ask Questions

Is there:

A command to obey

A promise to claim

A sin to avoid

An application to make

Something new about God

Ask: Who, What, When, Where, Why

Emphasize:
Different words

Rewrite:
In your own words

Best verse and thought for the day. (Write the verse & your thoughts.)

C*ommunicate With God*

W - *Worship Him*

A - *Admit Sin*

R - *My Requests*

Date ______________ Passage I Read Today ______________

Major themes from all I read.

Ask Questions

Is there:

A command to obey

A promise to claim

A sin to avoid

An application to make

Something new about God

Ask: Who, What, When, Where, Why

Emphasize:
Different words

Rewrite:
In your own words

Best verse and thought for the day. (Write the verse & your thoughts.)

Communicate With God

W - *Worship Him*

A - *Admit Sin*

R - *My Requests*

Date ______________ Passage I Read Today ______________

Major themes from all I read.

Ask Questions

Is there:

A command to obey

A promise to claim

A sin to avoid

An application to make

Something new about God

Ask: Who, What, When, Where, Why

Emphasize:
Different words

Rewrite:
In your own words

Best verse and thought for the day. (Write the verse & your thoughts.)

Communicate With God

W - *Worship Him*

A - *Admit Sin*

R - *My Requests*

Date ______________ Passage I Read Today ______________

Major themes from all I read.

Ask Questions

Is there:

A command to obey

A promise to claim

A sin to avoid

An application to make

Something new about God

Ask: Who, What, When, Where, Why

Emphasize: Different words

Rewrite: In your own words

Best verse and thought for the day. (Write the verse & your thoughts.)

Communicate *With God*

W - *Worship Him*

A - *Admit Sin*

R - *My Requests*

Date ______________ Passage I Read Today ______________

Major themes from all I read.

Ask Questions

Is there:

A command to obey

A promise to claim

A sin to avoid

An application to make

Something new about God

Ask: Who, What, When, Where, Why

Emphasize: Different words

Rewrite: In your own words

Best verse and thought for the day. (Write the verse & your thoughts.)

Communicate *With God*

W - *Worship Him*

A - *Admit Sin*

R - *My Requests*

Date ______________ Passage I Read Today ______________

Major themes from all I read.

Ask Questions

Is there:

A command to obey

A promise to claim

A sin to avoid

An application to make

Something new about God

Ask: Who, What, When, Where, Why

Emphasize: Different words

Rewrite: In your own words

Best verse and thought for the day. (Write the verse & your thoughts.)

Communicate With God

W - *Worship Him*

A - *Admit Sin*

R - *My Requests*

Date ______________ Passage I Read Today ______________

Major themes from all I read.

Ask Questions

Is there:

A command to obey

A promise to claim

A sin to avoid

An application to make

Something new about God

Ask: Who, What, When, Where, Why

Emphasize: Different words

Rewrite: In your own words

Best verse and thought for the day. (Write the verse & your thoughts.)

Communicate With God

W - *Worship Him*

A - *Admit Sin*

R - *My Requests*

Date ______________ Passage I Read Today ______________

Ask Questions

Is there:

A command to obey

A promise to claim

A sin to avoid

An application to make

Something new about God

Ask: Who, What, When, Where, Why

Emphasize:
Different words

Rewrite:
In your own words

Major themes from all I read.

Best verse and thought for the day. (Write the verse & your thoughts.)

Communicate *With God*

W - *Worship Him*

A - *Admit Sin*

R - *My Requests*

Date ______________ Passage I Read Today ______________

Ask Questions

Is there:

A command to obey

A promise to claim

A sin to avoid

An application to make

Something new about God

Ask: Who, What, When, Where, Why

Emphasize:
Different words

Rewrite:
In your own words

Major themes from all I read.

Best verse and thought for the day. (Write the verse & your thoughts.)

Communicate *With God*

W - *Worship Him*

A - *Admit Sin*

R - *My Requests*

Date ______________ Passage I Read Today ______________

Ask Questions

Is there:

A command to obey

A promise to claim

A sin to avoid

An application to make

Something new about God

Ask: Who, What, When, Where, Why

Emphasize: Different words

Rewrite: In your own words

Major themes from all I read.

Best verse and thought for the day. (Write the verse & your thoughts.)

Communicate With God

W - *Worship Him*

A - *Admit Sin*

R - *My Requests*

Date ______________ Passage I Read Today ______________

Ask Questions

Is there:

A command to obey

A promise to claim

A sin to avoid

An application to make

Something new about God

Ask: Who, What, When, Where, Why

Emphasize: Different words

Rewrite: In your own words

Major themes from all I read.

Best verse and thought for the day. (Write the verse & your thoughts.)

Communicate With God

W - *Worship Him*

A - *Admit Sin*

R - *My Requests*

Date________________ Passage I Read Today________________

Ask Questions

Is there:

A command to obey

A promise to claim

A sin to avoid

An application to make

Something new about God

Ask: Who, What, When, Where, Why

Emphasize:
Different words

Rewrite:
In your own words

Major themes from all I read.

Best verse and thought for the day. (Write the verse & your thoughts.)

Communicate *With God*

W - *Worship Him*

A - *Admit Sin*

R - *My Requests*

Date________________ Passage I Read Today________________

Ask Questions

Is there:

A command to obey

A promise to claim

A sin to avoid

An application to make

Something new about God

Ask: Who, What, When, Where, Why

Emphasize:
Different words

Rewrite:
In your own words

Major themes from all I read.

Best verse and thought for the day. (Write the verse & your thoughts.)

Communicate *With God*

W - *Worship Him*

A - *Admit Sin*

R - *My Requests*

Date ____________ Passage I Read Today ____________

Major themes from all I read.

Ask Questions

Is there:

A command to obey

A promise to claim

A sin to avoid

An application to make

Something new about God

Ask: Who, What, When, Where, Why

Emphasize:
Different words

Rewrite:
In your own words

Best verse and thought for the day. (Write the verse & your thoughts.)

Communicate *With God*

W - *Worship Him*

A - *Admit Sin*

R - *My Requests*

Date ____________ Passage I Read Today ____________

Major themes from all I read.

Ask Questions

Is there:

A command to obey

A promise to claim

A sin to avoid

An application to make

Something new about God

Ask: Who, What, When, Where, Why

Emphasize:
Different words

Rewrite:
In your own words

Best verse and thought for the day. (Write the verse & your thoughts.)

Communicate *With God*

W - *Worship Him*

A - *Admit Sin*

R - *My Requests*

Date ____________ Passage I Read Today ____________

Major themes from all I read.

Ask Questions

Is there:

A command to obey

A promise to claim

A sin to avoid

An application to make

Something new about God

Ask: Who, What, When, Where, Why

Emphasize: Different words

Rewrite: In your own words

Best verse and thought for the day. (Write the verse & your thoughts.)

Communicate With God

W - *Worship Him*

A - *Admit Sin*

R - *My Requests*

Date ____________ Passage I Read Today ____________

Major themes from all I read.

Ask Questions

Is there:

A command to obey

A promise to claim

A sin to avoid

An application to make

Something new about God

Ask: Who, What, When, Where, Why

Emphasize: Different words

Rewrite: In your own words

Best verse and thought for the day. (Write the verse & your thoughts.)

Communicate With God

W - *Worship Him*

A - *Admit Sin*

R - *My Requests*

Date __________ Passage I Read Today __________

Major themes from all I read.

Ask Questions

Is there:

A command to obey

A promise to claim

A sin to avoid

An application to make

Something new about God

Ask: Who, What, When, Where, Why

Emphasize: Different words

Rewrite: In your own words

Best verse and thought for the day. (Write the verse & your thoughts.)

Communicate With God

W - *Worship Him*

A - *Admit Sin*

R - *My Requests*

Date __________ Passage I Read Today __________

Major themes from all I read.

Ask Questions

Is there:

A command to obey

A promise to claim

A sin to avoid

An application to make

Something new about God

Ask: Who, What, When, Where, Why

Emphasize: Different words

Rewrite: In your own words

Best verse and thought for the day. (Write the verse & your thoughts.)

Communicate With God

W - *Worship Him*

A - *Admit Sin*

R - *My Requests*

Completion Record
Course Requirements for Book 2

This course is designed for men who want to become the man God wants them to be. Change will only happen when we do the work and give it our best effort. The *Completion Record* is a tool designed to help you gauge your progress and help you encourage each other to succeed.

Have another member of your group check you on the requirements of this course. Have them initial and date each item.

Scripture Memory Record

I have memorized and quoted word-perfect:

	INITIAL - DATE
Genesis 2:18	____________________
Ephesians 5:25	____________________
1 Peter 4:19	____________________
1 Peter 3:7	____________________
My Marriage Commitment	____________________
Three Biblical Principles on Raising Children	____________________
Ephesians 6:4	____________________
Proverbs 18:21	____________________
Proverbs 18:13	____________________
Quoted all of the above	____________________
1 Peter 3:8-9	____________________

Book 2: Marriage and Raising Children

INITIAL - DATE

Lesson 1: *Filling Up Gaps* ____________

Lesson 2: *The Godly Husband* ____________

Lesson 3: *When Marriages Hurt* ____________

Lesson 4: *The Wounded Wife* ____________

Lesson 5: *Turning the Hearts of Fathers to Their Children* ____________

Lesson 6: *The Tongue Has the Power of Life and Death* ____________

Lesson 7: *The Teenage Years: Who's in Control* ____________

Lesson 8: *Turning the Hearts of Children to Their Fathers* ____________

Quiet Time Journal Record

INITIAL - DATE

I have recorded ten Quiet Time sessions in my journal. ____________

I have recorded twenty Quiet Time sessions in my journal. ____________

Course Requirements for Completion of Book 2

- Finish all eight lessons. ____________
- Memorize and quote seven Scripture passages. ____________
- Learned My Marriage Commitment. ____________
- Learned Three Biblical Principles on Raising Children. ____________
- Recorded twenty Quiet Times or more. ____________

Congratulations! You have finished Book 2 of this course.

ABOUT THE AUTHOR: LONNIE BERGER

Lonnie Berger has been on staff with The Navigators, an international Christian organization known for its expertise in discipleship and leadership development, for more than 30 years.

While in college at Kansas State University in Manhattan, Kansas, Mr. Berger received his initial Navigator ministry training. His first staff assignment was behind the Iron Curtain in communist Romania, where he lived and directed the Navigator work in three cities. There he met his missionary wife, June, also ministering in Romania with The Navigators. They have been married since 1984 and have two grown daughters, Stephanie and Karen.

During his years on staff with The Navigators, Mr. Berger has served as one of five U.S. Directors for the Community ministry, overseeing the development of 175 staff in 125 major cities. He is a conference speaker and continues mentoring other Christian leaders in discipleship, evangelism, ministry funding, and spiritual warfare.

www.EveryManAWarrior.com

Every Man a Warrior is a ministry of The Navigators.